The dog, the hawk and I

The dog, the hawk and I

A walk through the year
in 100 columns
on the outdoors and nature

by KEN WEBER

The Providence Journal Company
Providence, Rhode Island

ISBN 0937550078

PHOTO CREDITS: Cover and frontispiece, Bob Thayer; page 23, Steve Haines;
page 38, Lynwood M. Chace; page 71, Jim Daniels; page 89, Ewing Galloway;
page 90, Constance Brown; page 113, John L. Hanlon; page 114, Steven Rock-
stein; page 121, Thomas D. Stevens; page 122, Lynwood M. Chace; page 137, Ed
Lincoln; page 138, Ewing Galloway; page 147, Lawrence S. Millard; pages 148
and 175, Providence Journal News Library; page 176, Reynold R. Paniccia; page
190, Andy Dickerman; page 195, Bob Thayer; page 196, Robert Emerson; page
218, U.S. Department of the Interior Fish and Wildlife Service; page 223, Providence Journal News Library.

For Bettie

For whom I seek the April bluebird
To whom I bring the wild rose
With whom I walk in autumn splendor
With whom I share the fireside glow
With whom I savor the twilight haze
For whom I cherish all the days

Table of Contents

Foreword

The man who wrote this book grew up on a farm in western Ohio, where the land is flat as a table top and farm boys learn to mark the seasons by the warm caress of a spring breeze and the smell of the earth when a furrow is turned by the plow.

Ken Weber left that farm years ago and headed for the crowded East. Reading this collection of delightful essays on nature makes it plain that he never really left that farm, that he brought his love for the land and the creatures that live on it and under it and above it with him to New England when he settled in the apple country of northwestern Rhode Island.

Mr. Weber takes the time in a complex and hurried age to see, feel, hear and smell the earth, the flowers, the birds of the air and the small animals that still roam southern New England away from the city lights, as he phrases it. Writing with a simple style that flows like a meadowland brook, he shares in this collection what his senses record. Those of us who have grown too far from nature will feel a tug at our own childhood roots that may have been nourished on other farms or in other small towns.

This book, Mr. Weber's own selection of 100 columns from the many hundreds he has written for the Providence Journal-Bulletin since 1971, is not a book you settle down with for a long stay. Rather, it is meant to be read in snatches, at any time, when you want or need a glimpse into the secrets and beauties of spring, or summer, or fall, or winter.

He begins his book with April (if he had his way, New Year's Day would be April 1, a time when the earth begins to burst with renewed life) and journeys through the year. We walk with him through the seasons as he notices sights and sounds and smells of outdoor life that still exists despite the inroads of shopping malls, residential developments and often unruly suburban sprawl.

He finds beauty in a walk through the snow and delights in summer rain. He glimpses a flock of geese heading south as winter nears, strolls a deserted beach in winter and chides a bunch of crow bullies for harassing a tired old owl that simply wants to be left alone so it can sleep. His columns on the playful chickadees and juncos, those winter friends of ours, are especially enjoyable.

Mr. Weber obviously loves the variety of New England, with its brooks and hills and valleys. He appreciates the creatures that live there as though he had grown up in his adopted environment, yet he still makes an annual pilgrimage to the farm in Ohio that was cut out of a swamp by his great grandparents more than 100 years ago and where his parents still live. He tells about that journey, his ties to farmlife and about the days when he first discovered with wonderment the world around him.

This is his third book. In 1978, he published *25 Walks in Rhode Island*, which sold 10,000 copies, and later wrote *Canoeing Massachusetts, Rhode Island and Connecticut*, which is now in its third printing.

He does most of his roaming today with his golden retriever, Rusty, darting ahead of him. There are four teenagers — two sons and two daughters — and a wife, Bettie, at home in Greenville, Rhode Island, on land that not too long ago was an apple orchard.

Journeying with Mr. Weber through the fields and woods, across the ponds and down the rivers is a poetic experience.

Robert Frost would understand how best to read Mr. Weber's short essays. In his poem, *The Pasture*, as he headed out to clean a leaf-clogged spring, Frost wrote:

"I shan't be gone long — you come too."

Lawrence Howard
Associate Managing Editor
Providence Journal-Bulletin

The dog, the hawk and I

April 1 — New Year's Day

This is New Year's Day. The first day of the year. Okay, it's not. But it should be.

Doesn't it make more sense to start the year at a time like this, April 1, when life is bursting out all around, instead of in the middle of winter? What is there to look forward to after Jan. 1 except more snow and ice and bundle-up weather?

Even the "official" beginning of spring is a little off. It's tied to the equinox — that moment when the periods of daylight and darkness are equal — but that's a bit too early. In New England, March 21 usually falls during a cold, blustery, rainy time when even the chickadees have trouble finding something to be cheerful about. We've already had enough of spring's teasing by then, and are so eager to get to the real thing that the cold wind and rain are twice as miserable as they would be at other times.

But now it's April and we can realistically expect major changes. In fact, in April there is something fresh and invigorating happening every day. It really is a "new" year in the countryside. This is the day we should celebrate.

Tomorrow there may be tree swallows swooping over the ponds and lakes, putting on aerial acrobatics the likes of which haven't been seen here since the swallows' departure last fall.

The next day, there might be chipmunks back on the stone walls, chattering away as if making up for their long months of hibernation.

Soon, we'll find the first wildflowers blooming, and whether those "flowers" are longed-for hepaticas or those unwanted dandelions, we'll pause to look and maybe even admit how much color and vitality they add to the landscape.

More birds will be arriving almost daily. Flickers. Kingfishers. Brown thrashers. Orioles. And each one will add its voice to the dawn serenades. Listen to that outpouring of song and just try to feel indifferent about it all. It's not possible.

The grass grows greener by the day, and even though that means we'll soon have to get the mowers working again, most of us will realize how much we missed that greenery. Suddenly, we know that the world just doesn't look quite right without green, the color of life itself.

Buds will be popping open and seeds sprouting and tiny bodies stirring again in pupa and egg. There will be bees and butterflies in flight once again, performing age-old tasks that are miracles in their own rights. Just seeing them reminds us how much is beyond our understanding, but worth our admiration.

Not all of this will be triggered by flipping a calendar to April 1, of course, any more than March 21 turned the seasons from winter to spring. But if we must have a date for starting something, a "new" year, a line of demarcation, then this should be the day. The year will never be newer than right now.

Happy New Year!

Can't work now; too much to do

The end of March and the beginning of April are such busy times. There's so much to do around the yard, so many tasks that must be done in preparation for spring.

Maybe I'll start by raking the pine needles off the strawberry patch. The needles protected the plants very well all winter; now it's time for them to be freed to enjoy the sunshine.

But first, I think I'll stroll down to the bog. The spring peepers are calling, and there's a strange clacking sound coming from the water. Is that a wood frog?

It's time to cut back the raspberry brambles beside the garden before they really get going again. Give them an inch and they'll take half the yard.

But that will have to wait a few minutes. I've heard that the phoebes have returned to the river bridge. They've nested under that bridge for the last 10 years. I'd better go and welcome them home.

My stone wall along the woods has tumbled in a few places; if we are through with heavy frosts this might be a good time to rebuild it.

But I can't disturb the area just yet. Violets grow beside that wall, and they'll be blooming soon. It would be a crime to stomp on violets just as they are about to bloom.

I should spread more fertilizer around the garden, and maybe scatter ashes from the fireplace across the flower beds. It's a way of giving something back to the soil, repaying it for all it gives us.

But that will have to wait until I get back from the marshy woods, where the red-winged blackbirds are gossiping up a storm. Wonder if the females, which always lag a few weeks behind the males, are back here yet.

The mud of February and March showed the need for a stone walkway back to the garden shed. Perhaps I should get that built now.

But a pair of ducks just flew by; could they be planning to

5

nest on the pond again? And with the reservoir now free of ice, the mergansers could be back. I'll have to drive over there for a look.

This might be a good time to build the cold frame I've been planning, a glass-topped box for starting tomatoes and other sensitive plants.

But the boys say earthworms are close to the surface, and they want to go fishing. I'd better tag along to make sure they haven't forgotten how to cast.

I have to clean up the buckets and spiles and the rest of the equipment we used in making maple syrup before storing all the gear away for the year.

But first, I'd better make the rounds of the birdhouses. Swallows could be arriving any day now, and wrens won't be far behind. Wonder if bluebirds have checked out the boxes I put up for them during the winter.

The car needs a washing and waxing after surviving another winter, and I should be getting the garden tools ready, and maybe even tuning up the lawn mower.

But I don't think I can squeeze those jobs in today. I have to see if the marsh marigolds are blooming yet, and whether the fox den up on the hill is being used this spring, and how many woodchuck holes have been cleaned out, and if the bees are stirring in their hive in the hollow tree.

There are so many tasks around the yard at this time of year. But I can't find time to do them. Other things are more important.

Peepers

It doesn't seem possible. How can something so small make so much noise? And how can something so loud and so common be so hard to find?

Anyone who lives outside the cities has been hearing the tiny tree frogs called spring peepers for a few weeks already. This is their time, and they're making the most of it. The din coming from the small bogs, marshes and woodland ponds these days is constant, a shrill chanting that can be almost deafening to a nearby listener.

But just try to see the little frogs. That's a different matter. They are so small — not much larger than a nickel — and blend in so perfectly with the decaying weeds stalks and leaves in the marsh water that they are all but invisible.

In fact, even after years of hearing them drone through April in the marsh behind our house, Bettie is not sure they even exist. Spring peepers are a figment of my imagination, she says.

We've gone out looking for them many times. We edge up close to the bog and take a comfortable seat on a rock or log, and stare into the water. We've even used binoculars. That not only greatly enlarges the images (whatever they may be) but enables us to focus on each individual cattail and stick and bubble in the water. And still she has never seen a spring peeper.

Obviously, the binocular trick doesn't always work. But that's how I first peeped into the peepers' world. Several years ago, I wandered up to a woods pond while searching for an owl. The frogs' chanting drew my attention and, since I had the glasses in my hands, I trained them on the weeds and brush in the water.

Suddenly, I saw a pulsating bubble, and realized it was the billowing throat sac of one of the frogs. When I discovered what it was that I was looking for, I began seeing the frogs all over the pool — on branches several feet out of the water, clinging to weeds just above the surface, and as bubbles in the water itself.

Since then, however, I have trouble finding them again. Occasionally, I see one swimming away, or I'll spot the slight ripple one makes in slipping off a perch. But I haven't watched one bellowing its shrill chant in some time. And it's frustrating.

Scientists say the call is actually a mating song, but listening to the tremendous racket always makes me wonder how the frogs can ever sort out the voices that turn them on from those that don't. But somehow they manage, and in just a matter of a few more weeks their ritual will be completed, the chanting will cease, and the peepers will slip back into oblivion for another year.

For now, though, the call of the little brown frogs keeps luring me down to the bog. Maybe the next time I go there that magical moment of years ago will return and I'll be able to watch peepers to my heart's content.

Maybe next time Bettie will even see one, and then she'll believe there really is such a frog, she'll realize I didn't really make up the story after all.

Our day for searching

It's become something of a ritual now, our way of paying homage to spring. When the temperature hits 70 for the first time, Bettie and I cancel whatever plans we have for the afternoon and go out looking.

Looking for what? Well, we look for swelling buds and awakening turtles and stirring bees and chanting frogs and tumbling brooks and returning birds. We go looking for spring.

There's a magic to that first day over 70, an aesthetic attraction that lures us outdoors just as does the first autumn morning after a hard frost and the first snowfall of winter. Such days should be holidays; offices and factories and schools feel like prisons.

This year, it was a long time coming. The first over-70 day — with the necessary brilliant sunshine and tugging breezes — didn't arrive until almost the middle of April. But it was worth the wait.

Red-winged blackbirds were clamoring in the treetops. Swallows swooped and dove over the stream. Spring peepers, the tiny woodland frogs, were shriller, louder than I ever remember them being.

The brook was rumbling and roaring like a wild thing unchained. The breezes kicked up leaves and tousled our hair as in March, but this time the touch was warm and welcome, instead of cold and cutting.

But best of all were the turtles. Probably nothing on this earth appreciates sunshine as much as turtles. It is life itself to them; they spend a great portion of their lives just soaking up the sunshine, and they disappear of necessity when that warmth is taken from them.

We went looking for them, too, heading for the "turtle log" in the backwaters of the stream. It's just a short log caught in a tangle of lily pads and other shallow-water vegetation, but the turtles love it. When spring comes, the log is their gathering place.

This time, it was jammed. We counted 28 turtles parked

9

there, shell to shell the entire length. I think all were painted turtles, the showy little creatures named for the myriad colors of their shells. Not one was moving. If we had been closer, I'm certain we'd have seen each one had its eyes closed, a picture of total contentment.

A short distance away, however, a turtle was anything but content. The sunshine had lured a monstrous snapping turtle out of the marsh and it was attempting to cross a road to the river. A car went by it on one side, and moments later a truck passed it on the other side. The snapper stood still, but swung its massive head from side to side in abject agitation.

Snapping turtles are anachronisms anyway, something left over from the age of dinosaurs with their hooked beaks and spiked tails and heavy armor. And this one looked like a patriach, being so huge — at least 20 inches across the shell — it must have been ancient indeed. Virtually invincible in the wild, snapping turtles can live to be 80 or more, and it seemed an injustice that this old warrior might meet death beneath the wheels of civilization.

So we helped it to the river. That sounds easier than it was, because snappers do snap, and this one continually lashed out at the stick I was using to prod it on its journey. Fortunately, it was a long, stout stick. They can easily chop through a stick the size of a man's finger, and they can do the same with the finger itself.

Eventually, it reached the shoulder of the highway, then half-slid, half-crawled down the slope to the water. It struggled through some shoreline brush, then gracefully swam away, sending up swirling clouds of dirt as it explored the river floor.

We watched for a few minutes, then headed home, satisfied in the knowledge that — for that moment — all was as it should be. The day was bright and the sunshine was warm and the turtles were back. We had found spring.

Spring on blue wings

The timing was perfect. Winter seemingly had returned, snow again covered the ground, the April breeze had turned into an icy gale, and spirits were about as bleak as the weather reports.

Then, a bit of sunshine and a flash of blue feathers, and suddenly all was right with the world once more. The first bluebirds can do that. They are spring.

Each time I see the first bluebirds of the season, the question again leaps to mind: What could be a more stirring blue? A June sky? A robin's egg? A quiet mountain lake?

No. There is no bluer blue; it's not even close. At least, that's the way it seems in April.

When the first bluebird arrives, appearing as if by magic on some fencepost or apple tree branch in these still-somber days well before leaves and blossoms, it's as if a new color has been invented all over again. Suddenly, it is evident the blue jays that raided the backyard feeders all winter weren't really blue at all. Compared with the bluebirds, the jays are gray.

Bluebirds are rare in New England now, victims of pesticide spraying and vanishing farmland and their own gentle dispositions — allowing more aggressive starlings and sparrows to take most of their hollow-tree nesting spots. Seeing any bluebirds at all is cause for celebration.

Once they were quite common, but as the open spaces dwindled and old orchards became housing developments, the birds were crowded out. Chemical pollutants, particularly in the days of DDT, further reduced the population. And then a lack of suitable nesting sites, due both to the starling's increase and our modern-day tendency to remove all dead trees, kept the birds from recovering.

So seeing the birds early in the year — especially this year — makes the event all the more rewarding. All they have to do is show up. They don't have to sing a note or snare their first caterpillar. Their presence is enough. That incredible blue of the male's back and wings, along with the rusty-red breast, fairly

11

shouts of spring. It stirs so much emotion in appreciative humans that it surely must stir sap in the orchard trees and breathe new life into the meadow plants. It has to be spring when the bluebirds come; it just has to be.

Our own first sighting came when we needed spring most. Only a day earlier, there had been reports of robins and other early arrivals from the south perishing in the blizzard. The ducks on the pond were being threatened by a widening sheet of ice. Swallows that had been swooping there the previous week had vanished, just as their prey, the hatching insects, had disappeared. The little frogs had stopped their chanting, retreating into the mud. We needed a bit of magic to bring it all back.

Then the bluebirds appeared. Typically, they were in a clearing near an old woods, and typically, there was a pair of them. They are the epitome of good citizenry among birds — faithful mates, devoted parents, guardians against insect pests, beautiful to listen to as well as to look at. If they have any bad habits at all, they've kept them well hidden.

Yet, they are so rare now that just seeing a pair brings one twinge of sadness along with the surging joy. Each time that blue flashes in the sun, I have to wonder: Is this the last time we'll see them? Are the bluebirds doomed?

I certainly hope not. Not after their timing this year.

A time to go back to

Every year, I try to make the trip. And every year I get asked why, why do I drive so far? I always give the same answer. It's a time to go back to.

A time — not just a place.

Each spring, I make the 1,600-mile drive to western Ohio and back. There are friends and family there, and the roots are deep. But I finally realized, it is not just the people I travel to visit. It is the time — early spring itself — that draws me "home." I just have to be there. To see it. Smell it. Hear it. Feel it.

It would be the same, I think, each autumn if I left New England. I'd want to come back for that moment when first frost hits, when the maples erupt into color, when wood smoke wafts through stirring breezes. Autumn just isn't the same anywhere else.

So it is with spring in the wide-open farm country. Plowing time. Planting time. Meadowlarks, just back from the south, singing from fenceposts. Winter wheat, so green it almost glistens, suddenly jumping up straight and tall after being weighed down for months by snow. Fruit buds swelling. Frogs chanting from the ponds. Barnyards full of young lambs and calves and colts and piglets and chicks.

There are no cities nearby to block the advance of spring; you can almost see it coming as you look over the endless horizon of fields and farms. The highway sounds are muted; you can hear the season approach. There is little pollution; you can smell the newly turned soil.

Perhaps I took it for granted when I lived there. Practically everybody does. But now I must go back to that time, go back and greet the meadowlarks, go back and say hello to the frogs, go back and take a turn around the field with the plow. Then I can stand there and know that the point has been passed, that spring has really arrived, where it is needed and appreciated most.

It is the time when every farmer envisions a perfect year. He works from dawn to dusk, but does so with optimism, even excitement, for he senses that now he can control his own destiny. Spring is the rebirth of the spirit as well as the land, but there, in that country, the two are practically one.

It is the time when every field yields a bumper crop, when every herd, every flock, multiplies with healthy, productive offspring. It is a time when it is again a privilege to live on the land, to work out in the sunshine and invigorating air. It is a time when nobody should be bound by walls and concrete and clocks.

It is a time to go back to.

Promise of the maples

It is a red haze now, a thickening cloud enveloping the maple forests.

And when those tree twigs begin glowing — as they are now — they trigger the splash of colors that will surge across the woodlands for the next six weeks or so.

Maples, of course, are known for their colors — the trees fiery foliage displays of autumn have long had poets struggling to find fitting adjectives. But their softer, more subtle, colors of spring may be just as significant, just as delightful.

When the maple buds burst, crimson florets "bloom" and create the current aura on the hillsides. Taken individually, the florets are not particularly impressive. But countless thousands of them, seen across a meadow or along a stream, produce a warm glow, and a warm feeling. They almost shout with promises of buds and blossoms, of leaves and growth.

This is a time when changes are happening so rapidly in the outdoors — the first wildflowers blooming, the new arrivals among the birds, the emergence of insects and reptiles — that less spectacular things often are overlooked. Not many people notice the early maple glow. But it means so much.

It means the dogwoods soon will be gowned in white blossoms. It means peach trees and plum trees are ready to flower. Next will be the apple boughs, and all the mountain laurel and rhododendron that is scattered through our woods.

It means there will be violets and dandelions, bluets and marsh marigolds, wild strawberry blossoms and lilac perfume. Plants will be flowering all over the countryside, in the meadows and marshes, in the forests and fencerows.

And it means the maples themselves are revived, shaken awake by the spring sunshine. After the florets serve their purpose, they'll tumble to the ground, and will be replaced by infant leaves. Eventually, those leaves, too, will grow, fulfill their mission, and develop into the foliage spectacles that we admire so much every October.

But all that splendor — the orange and gold and scarlet — is half a year away. It's even a few weeks yet until the green curtain of leaves will be dropped. That's okay, though. There's no hurry. Not now.

For now, it's enough that the florets, and their crimson haze, are here. They are the promise.

King of the waterways

Fishermen swarming along the rivers and ponds feel fortunate if they're successful a couple of times a day. But there is one bird out there that seldom misses when he goes fishing — maybe that's why he's called the kingfisher.

Anybody who has spent time prowling the stream banks, or paddling a canoe, or even picnicking beside a pond, knows the kingfisher. It makes sure of that. It's a flashy, noisy, entertaining bird that makes no secret about its presence, or its opinions about yours. The waterways are his; you are the intruder.

Kingfishers have been likened to overgrown blue jays, but it's not a good comparison. They do have somewhat similar blue and white color patterns (although male kingfishers have a regal red sash that no jay ever wore) and both species have crests, but there are few other similarities.

Blue jays are greedy, gluttonous bullies that sometimes seem to have no other mission in life than to clean out backyard feeders. They frequently attack smaller birds' eggs and young, and harass larger birds such as hawks and owls unmercifully. Their "song" is a harsh, grating scream. To blue jays, life apparently is one long headache.

Kingfishers, on the other hand, seem to have a rollicking good time from the day they arrive in spring to the time they finally head south late each fall. They can't sing either, but their call — a long, loud, rattling cry — is more a hallelujah, a declaration of triumph, than a complaint. They are the spirit of April, just as the raucous red-wing is the symbol of March and the sweet-singing oriole is the soul of May.

Kingfishers like the spotlight. They poise on tree limbs above the river, or hover in midair, and then plunge headlong into the water. More often than not, they come up with a fish. When they are successful, they swallow their catch, then proudly proclaim their own abilities. And if they don't connect, they launch into an excited cackle, explaining to all the world about the big one that got away.

Once the birds were considered pests by trout fishermen, who thought the kingfishers were taking more than their share of fish, and a great many birds were killed. Fortunately, we've learned differently — their take has no significant effect on our trout-fishing — and they are now protected by law. They are too appealing for us to begrudge them a few fish anyway.

Kingfishers seem to take particular delight in teasing canoeists. They fly a short distance ahead each time a canoe comes near, usually just going around a bend in the stream, then wait for the canoeists to catch up again. The game goes on and on, sometimes for miles.

Soon, kingfishers will have to get down to serious business. At nesting time, they dig long tunnels into cliffs or high river banks, often working on the task several days, and then will lay their eggs.

Feeding the young will be a full-time job for the parents, but they're never too busy to greet a fisherman with that rattling protest, and they'll still put on their shows for the boaters.

They're back now, setting up shop for the spring and summer, and they want everybody to know it. The kingfishers are many things, but shy they are not.

Farewell, old friends, and thanks

Nearly every day now, we greet new arrivals from the south. Tree swallows. Flickers. Kingfishers. Thrashers.

They're more than welcome. They shake springtime awake with songs and cries and frantic activity. But while these birds are arriving, other old friends are quietly leaving.

Soon, the juncos and evening grosbeaks will be seen no more. And virtually nobody will notice they are gone. When thrashers serenade us from the treetops and orioles flash their brilliant colors in the sunlight, who will miss the little gray junco? They might not be thought of again until next fall, when the orioles vanish once more.

But we owe the juncos and the grosbeaks much. They serve an invaluable purpose. In fact, it seems they might have been created just to fill that void that exists when other songbirds desert us each winter.

When the leaves fall and the cold winds start blowing, the swallows and tanagers and thrushes disappear. We are left with just a few hardy birds, mostly birds that look gloomy and act the same way — starlings, crows, sparrows. The jays have some color, but sour dispositions. Titmice and nuthatches are more congenial, but are too timid, preferring the deep woods. Only the chickadees of our native birds remain cheerful and lively through the bleak months.

That's where the juncos come in. They seem to love the winter. No matter how much snow there is, they continue to chirp happily while scratching around for weed seeds or helping themselves at the feeder. They show up every day; they'll be there when even the chickadees can't be found. We can always count on juncos.

Evening grosbeaks are far more colorful — almost gaudy with their yellow, black and white markings — but far less dependable. And maybe that's their contribution. Getting the grosbeaks to come to their feeders is a big challenge of many people. A flock of them will clean out your sunflower seed supply in a

19

hurry, but they'll add enough color and dash to the yard to make the winter pass far more quickly.

Yet, they're frustrating because the flocks often disappear for weeks between visits. So you keep waiting and watching, and each time that flock arrives, it's a small triumph. In winter, we need such triumphs.

Now, robins are in the yard and phoebes are singing and red-wings are calling from the marsh. You have to look hard to find juncos and grosbeaks. They've already faded into the background. Soon, they'll be heading back north. Their job here is completed; they're not needed anymore.

A few days ago, a single grosbeak dropped into our yard — first one to be there in a month — and sat on top of the feeder for several minutes. It seemed to be paying its respects, saying a silent goodbye. It left without even taking a seed.

It won't be long before the juncos depart as well. Their replacements are on the way. But the juncos served us well; they helped us get through the winter.

Farewell, old friends. And thanks.

Watching the day begin

The boy loves to fish. His father likes to watch the sun come up. A perfect combination — fishing as dawn arrives. The fishing may or may not be better then, but the fringe benefits are immeasurable.

Almost immediately upon being awakened at 4:15, the boy hurries down to "check the temp" and report that it's 31 degrees out. He's told to dress as if it's mid-winter, and the two try to leave the house without disturbing the female members of the family. They don't understand getting up before the sun. Not on a Saturday.

The dog does, though, and whines in disappointment when told to stay behind as they head for the car, already loaded with rods and tackle and with the canoe lashed firmly on top. There's ice on the windshield.

Even though the sun is not up yet, it's not really dark, and the boy breathlessly expounds on how "neat" it is to be able to see without daylight. Heavy clouds, blue and deep purple, cover much of the sky, creating shadowless, shapeless forms from the shrubs in the yard.

On the short drive to the pond, the father wonders whether they picked the right day. The clouds could obliterate the sunrise; the temperature may be too cold for the boy to enjoy his first pre-dawn fishing trip.

Already, there are others fishing. Two men are beside a van, casting from shore. Neither speaks as the father and son unload their canoe and gear. Perhaps they just arrived; if they had been there all night they would have a campfire going.

The water is smooth. They paddle around a point and head away from shore. As the boy baits his hook, the father notices a muskrat swimming ahead of the canoe, leaving a long V ripple behind. As they watch, the animal decides the pond is too wide to cross and turns back.

Crows are calling loudly from the hillside, which in the eerie light appears as wooded and wild as those in northern Maine.

21

There are other birds calling, too, and somewhere in the distance a woodpecker already is rapping industriously on some hollow limb.

There is a faint, far-away rumble of traffic, even at this hour, and somewhere a dog is barking. But on the pond, there is only silence, and the boy whispers instead of talking aloud. He asks how deep to set his hook, and the father lets the boy decide where he should anchor the canoe.

The sun hasn't popped out yet, but mist begins rising from the water. As it does, a lone Canada goose appears, resting contentedly near the far shore. Occasionally, a swallow swoops by. The fishermen wonder what the swallow is chasing; it's too chilly for insects to be out.

After a couple of nibbles, the boy hooks his first fish and proudly reels in a yellow perch. As the father takes it off the hook, the boy says yellow perch are among his favorite fish. "They're so pretty," he says, "and they feel so good; nice and plump."

Pink tinges are growing around the clouds just above the eastern horizon, and as a soft golden glow hovers over the hilltop, the fishermen pause, ready for the sunrise. But just at the wrong moment, a huge black cloud moves in.

There are more trucks on the highway now, and the increasing light reveals another father and son fishing from the right bank. Lights are blinking on in a few houses along the shore, and as more mist rises, more homes and streets are unveiled on the hillside. It's not Maine after all; it's Rhode Island.

The canoeists paddle into a narrow cove, and the boy pulls up two bluegills in quick succession. Patches of blue sky can be seen straight overhead, but the clouds still reign in the east. There is no sunshine.

They've been on the water two hours now, and the cold is seeping into their feet. They begin thinking and talking about breakfast. The boy says he's "gonna have C," which at their favorite diner in town is blueberry pancakes. The father says they'll be home before the rest of the family is up.

The trip hasn't been a total success. The boy was hoping for more than three little fish. He wanted at least one bass. And the father didn't get to see his sunrise across the pond. But neither is too disappointed. They saw muskrats and geese. They heard

22

crows and woodpeckers. They saw blue clouds turn gray. They saw mist lift a curtain on the pond.

They saw a day begin.

And they have an excuse for going back again. They plan to be out there again next Saturday.

May is...

Today is the first day of May, the beginning of a new month. But May is more than a month; more than 31 days on a calendar.

In a very real sense, May is a whole season unto itself. It is that special.

May is open windows and lilac perfume on the breezes and bees humming at the tulips.

May is roaring lawnmowers and Little League baseball games and small children reinventing dandelion necklaces.

May is tiny but succulent wild strawberries hiding in the meadow grass and the promise of summer displayed in the blossoms of the apple orchard.

May is orioles singing high in the treetops and migrating warblers passing through in waves and fuzzy ducklings already paddling around the pond.

May is violets blooming shyly at the woods' edge and daisies swaying in the fields and bluets so thick they resemble snowbanks.

May is long-legged colts in the pasture and fragrant first hay awaiting the baler and furrows plowed straight and deep.

May is a dawn chorus of a thousand birds in full song — the thrashers, the thrushes, the towhees, the tanagers, the grosbeaks, the meadowlarks.

May is rain-scrubbed sky the color of the robin's eggshell now discarded on the lawn, and a hillside of a hundred shades of pastel green that change day to day.

May is a boy with a fishing rod walking to the pond on Saturday morning, and young sweethearts strolling along the pond on Saturday night.

May is baby raccoons in the moonlight and woodchucks whistling from the hillside and chipmunks scurrying along the stone walls.

May is a canoe trip down the river and the family picnic in the park and toddlers getting their first rides on the swings.

May is the first mosquitoes but also the first bluebirds, the first poison ivy but also the first suntan.

May is time willingly spent in the garden, planting tomatoes and sweet corn, squash and cucumbers, and time grudgingly spent at indoor jobs when the mind is attuned to the sunshine.

May is polliwogs in the marsh and painted turtles soaking up the new warmth and the forgotten moment of terror always felt upon seeing the first snake of the year.

May is the instints of parenthood so strong in kingbirds that they drive away much larger hawks and crows, but nonexistent in cowbirds, which lay their eggs in other birds' nests and promptly forget them.

May is butterflies over the meadows and dogwoods in dazzling white gowns and infant leaves hungrily reaching for the benevolent sunshine and rain.

May, at its beginning, is warm jackets in the morning chill, and at its end, vacation plans and barefoot walks on the beach and a green world already knee-deep in summer.

May is surging life all around — life awakened and life returned and life bursting with growth. It is a time for all things living, a time for celebrating our own existence.

Truce with the woodchuck

My grizzled old neighbor, the one I call my friendly enemy, is back again. At dawn and dusk I see him in the meadow beyond the fence, catching up on all the eating he missed the last few months.

He's a woodchuck, up and around again after his long winter hibernation. He is hungry, too, and therefore a little less cautious than he will be later on. In midsummer I'll hardly know he is nearby, as long as he keeps the peace.

We have a truce of sorts, this woodchuck and I. As long as he stays on his side of the meadow, and away from my garden, he's in no danger from me. There will be no shooting or poisoning. But the garden is private property, and if he crosses the line he'll be in trouble.

Maybe he knows that, because for the last three years he has lived out there by the stone wall without disturbing the vegetables. He really has no need to bother us, though, for he has a whole field filled with clover and grasses and woodchuck delicacies of a hundred kinds.

Once last spring I thought he had broken the treaty when several of the tulips beside the garden path were being eaten off at ground level. I was ready for a showdown, until a pair of rabbits got caught in the act.

At this time of year, most woodchuck males are wrapped up in fierce mating battles, but my 'chuck is apparently a confirmed bachelor or past that stage of life. He has been alone all the time he has been here and seems to have no interest at all in the chucks that live several hundred yards farther up the slope.

After living off his fat since last fall's freezeup, it would seem the woodchuck would be skin and bones by now, but he isn't. He may not be as round as when he was stuffing himself in October, but he's still plenty plump.

He doesn't really burn up that much energy during hibernation, of course, for that is the next thing to being dead all winter. His breathing slows down from 260 breaths a minute to about 14, and his body temperature slides from over 100 degrees to 57. He seals himself into one chamber of his burrow and is completely oblivious of the world around him for the entire winter.

Now, though, there is a fresh mound of dirt around the burrow's entrance. Spring house-cleaning has begun. Whatever the force is that triggers his mysterious revival has worked again. He again climbs on that mound for a look around before waddling off into the meadow. Everything is just the same, except that the whiskers look a little whiter. And it's good to have him back — as long as he stays out of the garden.

Resurrection in the orchard

The annual resurrection of blossoms in the old apple orchard was more satisfying, more appreciated, this year than ever before. I thought they were gone forever.

Back in December, an ice storm left much of my area nearly paralyzed for several days. It also left me nearly in tears when, a week later, I discovered the terrible destruction that storm had wrought upon the forgotten orchard. To me, that collection of gnarled, disfigured trees meant much more than something to eat or sell.

That orchard, planted long before I was born and abandoned before I moved here, was one of my ties to an old New England I never knew, but one I feel I would have loved.

It had the stone walls that are so common in New England, but which are so unceasingly amazing to me for their workmanship and stability.

It had the tiny family cemetery hidden back in the corner, a final resting place that really was restful, surrounded by lilacs, wildflowers and apple trees.

It had the hilltop view of a little valley. It had the cellar hole of a long-ago house. It had the stirring breezes, the inevitable rock ledge, the gurgling brook, the birds.

It had everything a New England countryside should have. History. Beauty. Serenity. And apple blossoms.

But I thought the blossoms would be gone after viewing the wreckage from that ice storm. The old trees that had so bravely defied wind and insects and disease — and the most deadly of enemies, the years — seemed to have finally been conquered.

Not a single tree escaped damage. Trunks were split top to bottom on some. Twisted, mangled branches littered the ground. Huge limbs hung at grotesque angles.

I was sure I'd have to be content with just the stone wall and birds and breezes now, but the old trees fooled me. They blossomed again, even in their crippled condition.

Not all the branches made it, of course. Those severed from

the trunks still lie on the ground, never to blossom again. But many others, splintered and twisted though they are, somehow kept the spark of life.

I noticed that life when buds appeared in March, but was almost afraid to hope the blossoms would reappear. But they have, and even though the old orchard still shows scars that can never heal, those pink and white blossoms have made me appreciate the place more than ever.

I hope I'm not here when the trees no longer bloom.

Fishing

Fishing will never die out as a pastime. And it shouldn't.

There are people who fish for food, of course, but it's more than that. It's matching wits with an elusive trout or wary old bass. It's trying your skill at tying flies and jigging lures and casting lines against an unseen opponent. It's the excitement of the big strike, and the quiet waiting; the search for that perfect new spot, and the return to favorite old pools.

But, in reality, the fish may be only a small part of fishing. Most fishermen are too perverse, too practical, perhaps too self-conscious, to admit it, but it is other things that draw them to the ponds and streams and rivers. Fishing, for many, is only an excuse.

Now that the usual chaos of early season is past, the "real" fishermen are out there.

They listen to the plop of the plug, and the smooth whir of the reel, but they also hear the rattling cry of the kingfisher and the shoreline serenade of the oriole.

They keep a sharp eye out for darting fins as they paddle or wade through shallow water, but they also notice the shine on a dragonfly's wings and the colorful pattern of a painted turtle's shell.

They know the weed patch where the lunkers lie, but they also know the mallards back there now have a dozen fuzzy ducklings following them.

They might outwardly consider the gangly blue heron a rival for the fish, but deep inside they appreciate the bird's patience and skill, and probably even welcome its companionship.

They say they have to be out early, often before dawn, because the fishing is better then. Those in tune with their surroundings also know they may hear the last echoes of the whippoorwill's nighttime chants and the first greeting of the day by the irrepressible brown thrasher. They will see dawn mist rising from the ponds as the world awakes and dew shimmering on the grass and buttercups set aglow by the rising sun.

31

They will cast and drift and watch plastic bobbers. They'll be ready if a bluegill or rainbow or largemouth hits. But, in the meantime, they will notice the lazy passage of a fleecy cloud, the gradual travel of a maple tree's shadow. Morning on the water is special, but it doesn't stand still.

Too few of us are able, or willing, to shake free from other duties and commitments and schedules to spend a whole day fishing, but those who can are to be envied. Time spent on the water should not be hurried. The true fisherman is part of the scene. The sandpipers and bullfrogs pay no attention to clocks; why should the fisherman?

Unfortunately, we've been conditioned to think of watching clouds and listening to thrashers and admiring kingfishers as "wasting time," so fishing was invented. It gives the day a purpose and the fisherman an excuse to be out on the riverbank on a spring morning.

Understanding

This is the time of spring rituals — the first day of trout fishing, opening day at the ball park, migratory bird counts — but to the countryman, spring means planting. And understanding.

It means opening the winter-crusted sod. It means putting in seeds once more, renewing a partnership with soil and sunshine and water. It means helping initiate the miracle of germination and growth.

This opening of the earth, whether plowing mile-long furrows or spading up vestpocket vegetable gardens, is fundamental to those who live with the land. In fact, it may be the simple act of plowing — rather than the actual planting — that revives the sense of satisfaction that countrymen feel at this time of year.

There is a fragrance to freshly-turned loam — earthy, elemental — that is like no other. Few farmers or even gardeners will admit it, but for many it is that smell alone, that air of freshness and freedom and promise, that makes plowing such a favorite chore.

For others, it can be the feel of the soil. That, too, is unique. It, obviously, is much different here in stony New England than in the nutrient-rich midwest, but wherever men plow or spade, the scene is the same — long, frequent pauses to reach down, pick up a clump of dirt and crumble the soil between thumb and forefinger.

What is that supposed to tell you? I'm not sure. Maybe it's a test to see if the moisture content is just right for planting. Maybe a farmer can tell from this how long it will be until germination. And maybe he handles the soil just because it feels good.

That's my reason. But perhaps it goes deeper than that. Something in my heritage requires me to not only put out a garden each spring, but to do it by hand. I use a spade and battle the rocks and, every so often, pause and pick up a handful of soil.

My father, in his 80s, is probably still using this test. He always did. Feeling the good dirt, he called it. So did his father, and his father's father.

They all worked the flat, open farmland of Ohio. They tromped along behind teams of horse, maneuvering around stumps in newly cleared fields. They rode clanking tractors and sliced long, deep furrows that stretched into the next county. They plowed half an acre a day, and they opened entire fields in a day. Equipment and techniques changed, but the satisfaction remained the same.

My garden is insignificant, indeed, by comparison. Yet I feel a strong link, a deep sense of kinship, with those men each spring.

The fragrance of the new soil is just as invigorating. I, too, can watch robins swoop in and attack the exposed earthworms. I, too, can dictate what will grow where, provided, of course, that I keep up with the weeds.

But best of all, I am reminded of what countrymen everywhere realize, that is the land itself that produces the bounty of summer. It is the land and the sunshine and the spring plowing and planting and the miracles of the seeds. That understanding is essential, and it comes easily to a man with a clump of soil in his hand.

A delight by any name

He goes by several names — towhee, chewink, ground robin, joree — but whatever you call him, he's a delight. There aren't many birds as friendly, as cooperative.

He not only lets people hear him and see him, he seems to enjoy traveling along with us humans.

Towhees are long-tailed songbirds of the woods edges. They spend most of their time near the ground, scratching around for spiders and crickets and other creepy, crawly goodies.

In May, though, towhees — the jaunty males in particular — are just as busy calling out to each other and to the people who wander by. Other birds often lapse into silence when people come by, but not the towhees. They let you know where they are, and will even escort you down the trail aways.

Because they prefer forest edges — deep woods are for more timid birds, such as the wood thrush — you'll often find them along the paths. Which is perfect for their personalities. They like to keep tabs on the comings and goings in their area.

Canoeists see them, too. Towhees are in and under the bushes at the shore, and they'll call to the paddlers as they pass. Sometimes they'll fly along, a few yards at a time, and keep up the chatter until the canoe passes into the next towhee's territory.

The names towhee, chewink and joree are all various interpretations of the bird's two-syllable call. Towhee — rather *tow-HEEE!* — is probably the most accurate. The bird has another song, with several notes, used in courting, but it's the two-note call that rings through the countryside these days.

The male does resemble a robin — hence it's other name — but is more sharply colored, a glistening black head and neck, clear white breast and belly and robin-red sides. He's about the size of a robin, but slimmer, and the tail is longer. The female is nearly as bubbly in disposition but less conspicuous in appearance, being a soft brown where the male is black.

Later, the towhees will have more serious business to attend to. They're among the primary victims of cowbirds, the despicable free-loaders that lay their eggs in other birds' nests. Many towhee nests will contain at least one cowbird egg, and when the young are hatched, the greedy little cowbirds will gobble more than their share of the food, and often they'll crowd the baby towhees right out of their own nests.

But that time is ahead, and right now the towhees don't seem to have a care in the world. They strut across the paths, flipping those long tails. They scratch around the old leaves like miniature roosters. And they call out their greetings to all who pass their way.

Whether that call is *tow-HEE* or *che-WINK* or *jo-REE* makes little difference. It's just good to be hearing it again.

C'mon owls; just once...

Just once I want to see an owl retaliate. Just once.

At this time of year, crows are mercilessly tormenting owls that want only to sleep. It seems a bit unfair to me.

Whenever you hear a flock of crows making an unusually wild racket, you can be pretty sure they've found an owl. Occasionally, they'll gather around a hawk, too, but hawks are a bit more active in daylight, and might fight back, so the crows prefer owls.

And the crows always operate in flocks; bullies usually need gangs. A lone crow will call for reinforcements before venturing too close. Any owl could handle a crow with one talon tied behind its back if it wanted to.

The crows swarm around the owl, which is trying to snooze in some pine or hemlock, and harass it for hours. If it flies away, they'll follow, jeering and taunting at the top of their lungs, and sometimes dive-bombing — from behind, of course. Only rarely will the owl strike out at them; it just wants to be left alone.

Why do crows hate owls so much? Obviously, they have built-in grudges of some sort. Maybe an owl somewhere in the past raided a crow's nest and the tale is repeated to every new generation. Maybe they consider owls rivals for food or nesting territories. Maybe they just like bullying something that won't fight back.

Bird experts say this mobbing of owls is a message — move on, big fella; you're not welcome here. And they say the crow flocks really are family units; usually the parents and their offspring from the previous year. Some family pastime!

These crows remind me of street ruffians, young toughs ganging up on a big but defenseless stranger that wandered onto their turf. They are all bravado and noise and arrogance. They know the odds are all on their side.

But, just once, I want to see a great horned owl come out and really let one of the crows have it.

Just once.

37

Legacy in lilacs

Every spring, during May, I make it a point to walk up on the hillside beyond the marsh. There is a special place there, and this is a special time. For now, the living legacy left up there briefly recaptures its old glory.

A cabin once stood up there, among the rocks and trees. A cellar hole remains, and a few stone walls, but the rest of the farm has been obliterated by the years and the surging vegetation. Except in May, when the lilacs bloom again.

That farm must have been abandoned 100 years ago, maybe longer, but the lilacs live on. Unruly and twisted, they are only descendants of the originals, I'm sure, but that doesn't matter. When those bushes burst into flower each May, the forgotten farm comes alive again. It's as if those farmers — the Browns — left something of themselves behind.

I know their name was Brown from the faded, weather-worn tombstones in a tiny cemetery tucked away in the brush. Dates on the stones show the family has been gone for more than a century. Had it not been for the stones — both in the cemetery and in the cellars and walls — nobody would know the family ever lived there. All other signs of their life have vanished. All but the lilacs.

In spring, I climb up there, sit on the stone wall, drink in the delightful fragrances and absently muse on what life could have been like when the Browns lived there.

It must have been difficult indeed for them to wrest a living from the stony slopes and damp lowlands. But, somehow, I think it was just as hard for them to finally yield in their never-ending battle with the rocks, to give up the land. I feel a strange kinship with them, and each time I'm up there I wonder if they eventually found success and contentment in their next home, wherever that was. I hope so.

The lilacs testify to a determined effort to add beauty to that rugged life. There are bushes on each side of the steps down into the cellar, and several bushes around the entrance to the graveyard. At both places, the bushes are either crippled, with much dead wood and broken branches, or dense, towering giants that have been growing unchecked for years.

I'm sure the bushes looked better when the farmer's wife tended them, but the aroma couldn't have been better than it is now. When those purple flowers open, each hint of breeze is heavily perfumed. I can tell halfway up the hillside if the lilacs are blooming. The fragrance drifts down through the thick jungle of junipers and cedars and other trees and bushes that long ago crowded into the abandoned fields.

To me, the lilacs symbolize the ambition and optimism of the people who planted them. Anybody who tried to farm that rock-ribbed hillside had to be tough and persistent. That's what the lilacs are. And only when they bloom for the last time will the Browns really be gone.

Mom and the blue-eyed Marys

I'm sure Mom remembers the blue-eyed Marys. Larry probably does, too. I know I do.

It was many years ago. My brother Larry was a budding young botanist who spent his spare time roaming the fields and woods. He was about 10 at the time, and nothing was more exciting to him than finding a new wildflower or unusual plant.

On that stifling hot afternoon he came running into the yard, gasping for breath as only one who has run half a mile through the woods can. He had just made a great discovery, and needed to share the moment with somebody before he burst.

Mom was in the backyard, hanging out the wash. It had been a long day for her, as most days were on that farm, and she was glad it was her last load of clothes she would have to hang up that day. Supper was nearly ready, Dad would soon be home from work, and the older boys were coming in from the fields. It was almost time to relax, and Mom was looking forward to it. Just sitting down was a luxury.

But Larry ran straight to her.

"Mom, guess what? I found a whole patch of blue-eyed Marys down by the crick. A whole bunch of them! C'mon, I'll show you where. Let's go right now. Please?"

Mom didn't know what a blue-eyed Mary was and right then she didn't care too much. She said it was suppertime and Dad was on his way home and the "crick" was too far away. She didn't mention how tired she was. Larry didn't give her a chance.

"Aw, please, Mom. We can have supper a little later, can't we? They're the first blue-eyed Marys I ever found. And they're so beautiful. We just gotta go, right now."

She did, too. After telling me to explain to Dad, she told Larry to lead the way and she followed. Across the pasture and its thistles. Through the hot, dense woods and its mosquitoes. Over barbed-wire fences that clutched at Mom's dress. Along a winding cowpath the followed the stagnant, foul-smelling creek.

By the time they neared the clearing where Larry said the

flowers were, Mom was wondering why she ever agreed to go. But Larry's enthusiasm was catching, and despite the heat and distance, she found herself growing more excited as she brushed the last briars out of her way and pulled the spider webs out of her hair.

Then, suddenly, they were in the clearing, and it was almost breathtaking. A broad carpet of the bluest blue and greenest green she had ever seen stretched out at their feet. While Larry jabbered, Mom stood and drank in the sight. She was so glad now that she had yielded to a little boy's excitement.

Supper was late that night, but noboby seemed to mind, not after we saw how the flowers had refreshed Mom's spirit. The next evening, we all went down there for a look. And in the succeeding years there were numerous other excursions the family shared. Mom and Dad decided a child's enthusiasm was something to cultivate, not discourage, even if the subject seemed insignificant at the time. We seldom got the "Not now; I'm too tired" response from them. Not after the blue-eyed Marys.

Almost dogwood time

Any day now, those swollen buds will burst open and the hillside will be gowned in white. Dogwood time is just about here. Any day now.

A year ago this weekend, the dogwood blossoms were at their peak, shimmering in the sunshine, but they're a little late this spring. Like everything else. Cloudy, chilly weather in March and April dropped the spring a bit behind schedule and it's hurrying now to catch up.

Dogwoods aren't the first trees to blossom — some of the wild cherries bloom earlier, and so do many of the ornamentals and the domestic fruit trees — but there is something special about the dogwoods. Maybe it is because no matter how many times I see a dogwood in blossom, I'm surprised all over again that such an otherwise insignificant tree can put on such a spectacular show.

It is a long time between Mays, and it is easy to forget the dogwoods. For the rest of the year — except for a period in autumn when they display red leaves and shiny, scarlet berries — the trees fade into obscurity.

But any day now, they'll be back on center stage.

The dogwoods on our favorite hillside all seem to be rather scraggly. They grow at the edge of a thick forest, and have a great deal of competition for sunlight. So only the side of the tree facing outward has many healthy branches; limbs on the other side are shriveled and anemic. That apparently is the rule rather than the exception with wild dogwoods. They are lopsided and gnarled and even grotesque in shape.

Except in May. When those glorious blossoms open, when those big, immaculate petals catch the sunlight, all dogwoods are perfect. There is no finer tree in the woods.

From a distance, a single dogwood in bloom resembles a soft, white cloud hovering among the new greenery of the surrounding bushes and saplings. But up close, that cloud becomes a spectacle, one that draws us to the hillside year after year.

43

Farther up the hill, hidden from view until we climb there, is a place we call Dogwood Glen. It's just a little ravine that is lined with dogwoods — isn't glen a more appealing word than ravine? — that becomes a place of wonder in May. So many white blossoms they dazzle the eye and boggle the mind. We always seem to speak in hushed tones there; the pristine aura of the grove demands respect, almost reverence.

Later, the far-reaching oaks on both sides of the glen will leaf out and cast the dogwoods into deep shade for much of each day. By then, the blossoms will have served their purpose anyway, and the petals will fall like giant snowflakes.

But that time is a few weeks off. Right now, the anticipation of dogwood blossoms is as keen for us as awaiting the first song of the orioles and the first taste of wild strawberries.

It's almost time. Any day now.

The strawberry watch is on again

There will be wild strawberries up on the hillside again after all. I can hardly wait.

For years, the little patch has drawn me each spring. Wild strawberries are probably the most prized of all wild fruit — partially, I'm sure, because they are the first to ripen — and I'd often wander off from my garden chores when strawberry season arrived.

But last winter, bulldozers and trucks reached the hillside, making way for another housing development. When checked a month ago, the strawberry plants that remained were brown, withered and lifeless. Much sand and gravel had been spewed over them. Exposure to the ice and wind had done the rest.

It was not a happy discovery, but neither was it surprising. Loss of a wild strawberry patch would simply be added to all the other losses suffered out here in suburbia. A nearby woodlot had been leveled and grouse no longer drummed beyond the backyard fence. Several old trees were removed for a lane and swallows no longer nested beside the stream. Since houses were built in an abandoned pasture, bluebirds are harder to find, and so are woodchucks and foxes and bobolinks and elderberries and some of the wildflowers.

Bulldozers come and wildlife diminishes; it's the way of "progress."

When they reached the strawberry patch, there seemed nothing to do but heave a sigh of resignation and go looking for a new spot. Perhaps, somewhere, there is an open hillside still safe from the wheels and blades of civilization.

But the strawberries have survived. The benevolent sunshine worked its magic. Almost overnight, the leaves sprang back to life, and a rich, lively green replaced the brown. And the trucks have finished their work — for now, at least. Most of the traffic will be some distance away.

So the strawberry watch is on again.

Each spring, I try to keep close tabs on the berries' progress

45

from blossom to fruit formation to ripeness. I want to be there when it's time to start picking — there is no sweeter fruit on this planet than the first wild strawberries of May. I have plenty of strawberries in my garden, but I'd rather have a quart of wild strawberries than four quarts of the domestic kind.

However, there is so much competition. Catbirds and robins and mockingbirds are watching that patch, too. So are chipmunks and squirrels. They'll know when the berries are ripe, and if I wait a day too long, they'll do most of the harvesting.

This year, though, I don't think I'll resent the catbirds and chipmunks taking the berries as much as before. The patch has survived — for another year — and for that I'm grateful. Just let me have one handful.

Master mimic

✓ 12-29-85

Sooner or later I'm going to catch on. The mockingbirds aren't going to fool me forever. Well, I hope not, anyway.

Last summer I heard a duck quacking plaintively on my roof. A duck on the roof? I rushed out and found a mocker up on the TV antenna, doing an incredible imitation.

A few days ago, it was the sharp "bob-white" whistle of a quail. That's really rare around our yard — it was worth a look outside. Again, it turned out to be that mockingbird. I think it was laughing at us.

There have been other times, too, when the mocker has mimicked various birds. One year, it sang the red-winged blackbird's tune two days before the first red-wing of spring. It regularly repeats the cardinal's whistle long after our cardinals, which hang around the yard all winter, retreat to the marshy lowland for their nesting.

At a time when so many bird species are dwindling, the mockingbird's rise to prominence in New England is a unique story. Once confined to the deep south — in fact, it was something of a symbol of the old south — it gradually expanded its range until it is now quite common throughout this area.

And it's not a bird that skulks around the woods. Hardly. Mockingbirds like being around people — they probably need audiences. Any suburban backyard is more likely to have mockers than the wildest, most remote sanctuary. Apparently, humans are easier to fool than raccoons and owls, and what's the point in quacking like a duck if there is nobody around to hear it?

Our mockingbirds are equal parts endearing and exasperating. They sometimes start calling at 4 a.m. in the summer, and they boldly help themselves to strawberries and other small fruit. But they repay us with their exuberance and cheerfulness, even it at times we mutter, "Aw, it's only the mocker," when we expect to find something else.

In recent years, the mockers have added something extra. Their fondness for the berries of multiflora roses has resulted in

47

the planting of dozens of the rose bushes all over the meadow beyond the yard. This year, those bushes fairly gleamed for weeks with the white blossoms. It was exquisite. All because the mockers dropped the seeds.

Another trait we like is their independence. They staunchly refuse to accept handouts at the feeder all winter. They'll perch in nearby bushes and jeer the chickadees and jays and juncos that hungrily gobble up the sunflower seeds. Then the mocker will fly off to their rosehips and juniper berries.

But, more than anything else, what makes the mockingbird so special is its talent for imitation. Cornell University researchers once recorded a mockingbird that rattled off the calls of more than 30 other species, and there has been a report of another mocker that spieled off 42 recognizable phrases of about 25 species in a 16-minute outburst.

They've even been known to greet other birds — say, blue jays or flickers — in their own language before the other birds have uttered a sound.

So maybe I shouldn't get frustrated when my quail or mallard turns out to be a mockingbird. Mockers certainly keep things interesting, and noisy, around here. And they plant roses, too.

Gift of the fireflies

Whether you call them fireflies or lightning bugs, they are the essence of summer. Watch them flash in the warm, soft darkness — tiny lights flickering across the meadows and lawns — and you just know the season of plenty has arrived. They are a gift.

Fireflies serve no practical purpose, of course. They're not as industrious as the bees, or as pretty as the butterflies, or as ecologically important as the moths and beetles and even those blankety-blank mosquitoes.

No, the world would not fall apart if fireflies vanished forever. Trees and flowers would still blossom. Birds would find enough other insects to eat. And the repellent manufacturers would not notice the difference. Only people would miss fireflies, people who appreciate the beauty of this unique little night-flier. And kids.

Sometimes, it seems fireflies were put on earth just for kids. Has there ever been a child who spent his summer in the country, or even in suburbia, who has not chased fireflies? How many thousands of fireflies have been captured in glass jars? How many pairs of fascinated young eyes have reflected the lightning bugs' flashes.

Several years ago, when my children were very young, we stopped at a motel while journeying across Pennsylvania. It had rained during the day, but the night was clear and exquisite. The air, scrubbed and cooled, carried the fragrance of new-mown hay in the surrounding countryside. And the fireflies were out in force.

The kids, who needed to run anyway after the long hours in the car, dashed about for half the night, capturing dozens of lightning bugs in plastic bathroom cups. They ran barefoot over the huge lawn, joining children of other motel patrons — strangers who quickly became friends — in a delightful celebration of summertime and darkness and freedom and the gift of the fireflies. I don't think my kids will ever forget that night.

I know I won't.

Scientists have long attempted to explain the firefly's strange light. It's a slow, practically heatless oxidation of a substance called lucifern in the insect's body. All sorts of theories have been proposed on why the bug lights up — ranging from mating rituals to warnings for birds — but only the firefly itself knows for certain.

But maybe it's not really necessary to explain the firefly. Maybe this is one insect that actually was put here just to make us feel better. Somehow, watching the firefly blinking on and off can make problems slip from the mind for a moment. It can soothe frazzled nerves just a bit. Watch parents some time when their kids are chasing fireflies; their faces show a mixture of relaxation and contentment. More gifts of the firefly.

Yes, it's just an insignificant bug with a light in its tail section. Birds and flowers and trees can get along without it. But there's no question all people who appreciate the night outside walls would be far poorer without it.

The gliders

It can be hard to find something good to say about vultures. They are homely and smelly and have the worst means of earning a living of all birds. But, oh, can they soar!

Vultures — sometimes they're called buzzards — are those big blackish birds that apparently were put on earth to clean up carcasses. Practically all of their food is carrion; these days that means animals killed along the roads. It's not a pleasant task, certainly, but a useful one.

Maybe that's why the vultures were endowed with their gliding abilities. Maybe it's compensation for having to be the world's street-cleaners.

The birds are perfectly suited for their jobs. Without a doubt, they are the ugliest bird in the country. Besides their gloomy black feathers, their heads are warty, knobby, bare and bright red. When perched, they hunch their heads into bony shoulders and stare, the personification of impending doom. No wonder people feel uneasy when they see a vulture watching and waiting.

But once it is in the air, the vulture is the picture of effortless grace. There might not be a better glider among our birds. It stretches out its wings — a wingspan of six feet is not uncommon — and rides the air currents for hours. Over rocky hills or flat fields, using thermals or updrafts, it seems to defy gravity as it floats on and on.

Scientists used to debate whether the vultures found their, ah, prey by spotting it while gliding or by picking up the odors. Now they say it's a combination of the two. Both their eyesight and their sense of smell are said to be extraordinary. Just as good as their gliding skills.

Unfortunately, the vultures' personal habits are less exemplary. Once, in another part of the country, I came across a vulture nest in a huge hollow log. The stench was incredible. In fact, it was that repulsive odor that gave away the birds' presence — I had to find out what smelled so awful. I never went back for a second look.

Not long ago, vultures were rare in New England, but in recent years they have been becoming more common. Like other southern birds — cardinals, mockingbirds, titmice — they have been gradually expanding their ranges and now it is not unusual to see them throughout our region.

Luckily, it is usually when they are high in the air that we spot them. I often feel a twinge of envy as I watch them soar among the clouds. I would love to be able to do that. If I were choosing what bird I would like to be, it would not be a vulture, but still, being able to drift across the sky, silently, effortlessly, is something man has longed for since he first realized he was earthbound and other creatures were not.

Just recently, a pair of vultures moved into my area, and they're welcome. There's always room for more birds, especially those with such grace in flight. On bright, sunny days, it can be a delight to watch them circle in the heavens. But I have no intention of looking for their nest.

The humble bumblebees

Bumblebees have had a bad press. They're pictured as fierce, dangerous creatures that should be avoided at all costs. It's a bum rap.

In reality, they are more like Ferdinand the bull. Remember him? He was supposed to be the meanest, orneriest bull the matadors ever saw, but all he really wanted to do was sniff the flowers.

Bumblebees are like that, too. They'll ignore you if you let them alone. They're not looking for trouble; they're more interested in gathering nectar and building up their colony. They're lovers, not fighters.

Bumblebees should be considered ideal neighbors. They're industrious, they mind their own business, and they are colorful enough to be thought of as handsome.

Yet, people are afraid of them.

One reason, I suppose, is that they are bees, and when people think of bees they think only of stings. They are often called yellowjackets and hornets, and I'm sure part of their reputation comes from this confusion with true hornets. White-faced hornets are quick to sting, and a healthy respect for them is advised, but bumblebees are far more tolerant.

I've come to admire the big, fuzzy, yellow and black bumblers that constantly patrol our flowers and fruit blossoms and blooming bushes. They resemble lumbering freight planes, with their slow, deliberate flights. But they can hover effortlessly, and dart surprisingly fast when alarmed or enraged. So I don't scare them or antogonize them. We often work side by side; they going about their business while I take care of mine. We get along just fine.

Some people may find their buzzing intimidating, as well. It's an ominous drone that might be interpreted as a warning. I prefer to think of it as a hum, their way of whistling while they work.

They can sting, of course, but that's simply a last resort.

They can sting, of course, but that's simply a last resort. They not only don't mind having humans around, they do their best to pretend we don't exist. When they are busy extracting nectar from, say, a rhododendron flower, we can — and have — brushed them off with our hands without having them turn on us. They aren't interested in fighting. Flowers are more important. It's only when their nests are disturbed that they really get irritated.

At this time of year, bumblebees are still trying to get organized for the new season. The queen, which survived the winter snoozing deep in a crevice somewhere, often establishes her nest underground. She sometimes moves into a hollow tree, or takes over a mouse's nest, but more often will find sanctuary in or under a stone wall or rock or log. And she is not shy about nesting around the house or outbuildings, moving in wherever she finds a crack. As long as there are flowers nearby.

Once the workers are hatched, the colony is in business. Bumblebees don't produce gallons of honey, as a hive of the smaller honeybees will, but they manufacture enough for their own use and to feed their young.

And they earn their keep by helping to pollinate a great many flowers and trees.

So they're not really so tough, after all. With enough flowers, and a safe nest, they'll happily spend the spring and summer with the blossoms. In utter contentment. Just like Ferdinand.

Call of the whippoorwill

The call cames across the valley just after sunset, or maybe we'll hear it in the quiet hours before dawn. The whippoorwill is back.

Nobody who has ever heard the call can forget it. It can be enchanting or irritating; strangely lonely and lovely, or downright monotonous. Whatever the feelings, the whippoorwill is part of the June night out beyond the city lights and suburban yards. In fact, at times, it is the June night.

Few people have ever seen this elusive, shadowy bird, and not many even know what it looks like. But if you spend any time camping in quiet woodlands, or live near hillside pastures, you're likely to hear the whippoorwills sooner or later.

Unfortunately, like so many other birds, the whippoorwill is not as common as it once was. Many countrymen who once complained of being kept awake by the insistent calling now long to hear the chant again. Mention the whippoorwill's call to oldtimers, and they'll smile knowingly. The call is a memory, a legend.

However, even the most appreciative of countrymen and campers have had nights when they've cursed the chant. The reptitious three-syllable whistle — vaguely translated as whip-poor-will — can go on interminably. A Connecticut naturalist once wrote that he counted more than a thousand successive calls one night, with never more than a few seconds between them. Get two whippoorwills calling to each other from across a valley, and sleep will be disrupted for hours.

The bird itself is rather unattractive, a bulky, nondescript insect-eater the color of dead leaves. Its coloring blends in so well with the forest floor that it virtually disappears when at rest during the day. And it stays there when laying eggs, not even bothering to build a nest.

But it is really the call — nobody would ever say it's a song — that makes people remember the whippoorwill. Unlike two other fabled cries of the skies, those of the Canada goose and the loon, which spin tales of wandering and distant places, the whippoorwill's speaks reassuringly of Grampa's farm and evening conversations on the back porch.

There are not many places here in southern New England where the call is still heard, but once in a while a whippoorwill will move in for the summer. People who go indoors as soon as it gets dark, and constantly have the air conditioner running, still may not hear it. But those who let the night air in can't miss it. And even though the calling may cost them some sleep, when fall comes and the chanting ceases, they will discover a void in their lives.

Again, it may be years before the whippoorwill returns, and it might even take a camping trip to some remote wilderness setting to find the call once more, but whenever it finally is heard again, it will bring with it those satisfying echoes of summers gone by. Somehow, things will suddenly seem just a little more relaxed, a little more as they should be.

The whippoorwill's call in the June night can do that. Is it any wonder old men always want to hear it one more time?

Proper hoe-leaning is an art

The recent grow-it-yourself craze that has struck suburbanites has brought a whole new crop of gardeners to backyard plots. And those beginners can be spotted immediately — they don't know how to lean on a hoe properly.

Anybody can stick a tomato plant in the ground and it might grow. Carrots, cabbages and corn also do nearly as well for the novice as for the veteran. But developing the proper technique for leaning on a hoe takes years of practice. Without it — effort, sweat and results notwithstanding — the worker is just a hobbyist, not a bona fide gardener.

My own potential for hoe-leaning was recognized early by my father, who, after watching me perform in a patch of potatoes, said he had finally found something at which I could become a world champion. I was too young at the time to note the sarcasm in his voice.

Perfecting my style over the years brought the conclusion there are nearly as many basic fundamentals involved as in, say, hitting a baseball. Stance, timing and concentration are all important, but no more so than the right attitude and mental approach. Age is not a critical factor, but size can be, although hoes can be made to fit the body. There are no regulations governing the length of hoe handles.

No hoe-leaner can get into top form until July, the mid-season of the growing year. By then, the excitement of planting has worn off, and the anticipation of harvest is still a few weeks off. In addition, those who garden for a lark are on the beaches, leaving their turnips to fend for themselves against the quackgrass.

That's when the true hoe-leaner takes his rightful place. He heads out to the garden nearly every day after work. His hoe's handle is smooth and worn, the wood salty from the sweat of his hands. Corners of the hoe blade are gleaming, both from the sessions with the emery wheel and from the countless plunges into the ground. The center is crusted with dirt. Hoe-leaners really do work, you know.

But the art itself is in the rest breaks. A skilled hoe-leaner doesn't sit under a shade tree. He doesn't go in for a drink or stand there wiping his brow and looking miserable. No, he merely hooks the handle under his right armpit, with the left hand on the end for a cushion, crosses his feet at the ankles, and leans. Crossing the arms or letting the right arm hang free to wave at passersby is optional.

To the accomplished hoe-leaner, the stance is second nature.

For it to be comfortable, of course, he needs to be the right height so that the handle will come just to his armpit, but even more important are his state of mind and the direction he is facing.

Despite weariness and perspiration, the hoe-leaner must be content — and look it. Even nonchalant. A worrier would never make a good hoe-leaner; he has to be able to think only pleasant thoughts.

And he must stand so that his view is of the area already hoed, not of the work ahead. That is what supplies most of the contentment and satisfaction. It can be discouraging to dwell upon the work still ahead, so all of us hoe-leaners have learned to turn our back and gaze at the job just finished.

Beginners may learn how to stand, and they may be able to fake the nonchalance, but until they automatically turn around for their rest breaks, they'll never challenge my world championship.

Do orioles ever get sore throats?

Now that it's June — the year reaching maturity after the frantic awakening of April and growth of May — there is time to reflect on some fundamental questions.

For example, why are the catbirds so numerous this year? It seemed they were late in arriving, but now they are everywhere in the woods. Has there been a population explosion? Why?

And what produced the fantastic display of dogwoods this year? Were they ever more stunning? Maybe last summer's defoliation of the taller trees by the gypsy moths had something to do with it. Could it be?

Are the mosquitoes really more vicious this year, or does it just seem that way? Do other adults have trouble remembering mosquitoes being a problem years ago? We always played outside in the dark — now I can't sit in the yard 15 minutes at night without being devoured. Why?

Judging from the blossoms, it's going to be a banner year for wild blackberries, but only so-so for raspberries. Why? And why do so few people bother to pick elderberries these days? They're easy to gather, and make great jelly, but nearly all are left for the birds. Why?

Is the mortality rate among young wild creatures greater now than a couple of hundred years ago? There are fewer predators around, obviously, but highways and cars are taking a terrible toll. Have you noticed all the dead foxes and raccoons and rabbits and skunks along the roads? Right now, the majority of them are youngsters that never learned the danger of the wheels.

Why are people so afraid of bumblebees? Is it because of their ominous humming? Or do they equate all bees with hornets and wasps? Sure, bumblebees can sting, if provoked, but they're like Ferdinand the bull; they'd rather spend their lives contentedly among the flowers.

And speaking of flowers, how do the ladyslippers, blooming now in the woods, manage to live as they do? They look so delicate, so fragile, yet year after year they thrive in places where few

59

other flowers can survive — in oak forests where they are not only cut off from sunshine but have to stand in thick carpets of old, leathery leaves as well. And they bloom for weeks. How?

Does anybody ever remember in March how tall grass can grow by June? Why does lilac time go by so quickly? And is there a more nostalgic smell anywhere than new-mown hay?

Where are barn swallows nesting now that there are fewer barns? Under bridges again? Where did they nest before there were bridges or barns? How about phoebes? They nest almost exclusively under bridges now. Why?

Do little boys still catch garter snakes? And fireflies? Will little girls gather wild daisies for Father's Day, as my daughters once did? Do kids still run barefoot after a rain, just to feel the mud between their toes?

Do the orioles, singing so enthusiastically these mornings, ever get sore throats? How about the turtles; do they ever get bored with spending all day soaking up sunshine? Are the herons, standing so still in the swamp, ever bothered by mosquitoes? Why not?

Such questions come fleetingly these days, between sips of a tall, cold drink while lounging in the lawn chair. And there's another one. Why do those weeds in the garden grow so much faster than the vegetables? That's not right at all.

We're even now, Chipmunk

A debt was owed. Now it is paid.

But the transaction may have strained our relationship past the breaking point. After all, we already had been providing our tenant with a home and protection. Now he demands our food, too.

He is a nameless chipmunk who entered our yard — and our lives — two summers ago, shortly after I built the stone wall he now lives under. We were delighted; chipmunks are pert, amusing little rascals who automatically brighten their surroundings with their scurrying about and frantic chattering.

We'd watch from the kitchen window as he prowled the meadow in search of seeds, often climbing a straggly weed stalk and riding it to the ground.

He'd make trip after trip to the wild chokecherry bush beyond the fence, each time stuffing his cheek pouches so full his head seemed to triple in size.

He'd scream his objections when robins came to the birdbath.

He'd stalk crickets like a lion stalking a gazelle.

He'd lick dew from the grass in the morning while we drank our coffee.

But if we stepped outside or even made a quick movement at the window, he was gone in one red-brown flash.

That was okay with us. He could stay beneath the stone wall, and we'd even chase the dogs and cats away, as long as he kept the peace.

He didn't.

Problems started arising that first winter, when we noticed he was raiding the bird feeder too regularly. Sunflower seeds weren't going to the cardinals and chickadees as intended; they were going down in one of those tunnels under the stone wall.

But then it got cold, and the chipmunk went into his hibernation. By spring, all was forgiven, especially after he awoke and went into the two-week chattering-screaming-scolding proclamation that we now recognize as the official end of winter. He was so full of life he just couldn't keep it in, and his exuberance rubbed off on us.

Last summer, he gradually grew bolder, sometimes coming out on the stone wall and watching the kids play nearby. One evening, he came up right behind me, when I was working in the garden, and stole a cherry out of our tree. We thought it was cute at the time. Not any more.

His taste for our fruit was whetted. Now he is hooked.

When we noticed our strawberries being eaten this year, we at first blamed the robins and spread a netting over the patch. Then we saw the chipmunk gorging himself one evening, and subsequent vigils proved he was the thief.

Still, we weren't that upset. We figured we owed him something for all the pleasure he had given us in the past.

But now the debt is paid. In full. And he still keeps collecting. He spent more time in the cherry tree in late June than on the ground. He's already helped himself to the raspberries, and I swear I saw him sizing up the blueberries the other day, just waiting for them to ripen.

Enough is enough. If he gets our blueberries, out he goes. We'll let him perform for somebody else. His price is getting too high for us.

Sonnet for the whorled loosestrife

Does anybody write sonnets honoring the whorled loosestrife? Are there any poems about the blue-eyed grass? Who goes out searching for the first maiden pinks?

Violets and wild roses and even daisies have long been revered, and hundreds of countrymen still count it as a sign of spring when they find the first hepatica, the first marsh marigold, the first buttercup. Even dandelions are so welcome — except by the lawn purists — after the bleakness of winter that few fail to note arrival of the golden blooms.

But by mid-June, the surge of plant growth is so overwhelming that another wildflower is just another plant. It is usually ignored. Thousands grow, bloom, wither and fade without ever being noticed by the human eye. They're hidden in the tall grasses and weeds of the meadow, or lost among the tangles of the fencerows, but many are just as colorful and lovely as the heralded flowers of early spring.

Right now, the blue-eyed grasses are in their prime, and there may not be a more pleasing shade of blue this side of the bluebirds. The whorled loosestrife has an unispiring name — it certainly doesn't roll off the tongue like buttercup — but its petals are the color of spun gold. The maiden pinks do have a dainty, delicate name, and an appealing appearance to boot, but like the others, they too are seldom noticed. It's all in the timing. I wonder if violets would get more than a passing glance if they bloomed only in June or July.

The parade of such plants — and who's to say if they are "weeds" or flowers? — will continue through the summer and most of the fall, but theirs is a life of obscurity. Coming in the next few weeks are chicory, black-eyed Susans, oxeye daisies, milkweeds, wild irises and day lilies. Then it will be hawkweeds, Queen Anne's lace, yarrow, purple vetch, joe-pye weeds and ironweeds. By autumn, the meadows and lowlands will be covered with goldenrods and asters. Are they weeds or are they flowers?

Sure, chicory can be a pest, because it will grow virtually

anywhere, but it seems wrong to knock something with such a delightful shade of blue. Black-eyed Susans are pretty enough to be flowers, too, but they're too common to really be appreciated. It's the same with Queen Anne's lace and joe-pye and ironweeds. Goldenrods are a particular nuisance to some people with hay fever and allergies, but they're still flowers, aren't they?

Perhaps it doesn't matter. The loosestrife and blue-eyed grass and chicory don't really need man's approval or appreciation. They and the other outcasts of the flower world have their own place in the natural scheme of things. The bees and butterflies know them. Some provide forage for larger creatures, too; some produce food for birds.

But all have one thing in common. Whether they are noticed or not, they will bloom, they will show their colors to the sun, and they will produce enough seeds to insure survival. They may have the last laugh on man yet.

Poetry in motion

Just as the early-arriving tree swallows have always been one of the symbols of spring for me, so are their cousins, the barn swallows, the birds of summer.

I cannot think of barn swallows without seeing in my mind's eye their graceful swooping flights over hay fields and meadows just before dusk. When I was a boy mowing that alfalfa and clover, the swallows kept me company, their twisting, turning bodies flashing orange, gold, blue, black, white and half a dozen other colors in the late-afternoon sunlight.

The swallows seemed so in tune with the roar of the tractor and the clatter of the mower I'm surprised to this day whenever I watch their aerial shows and notice they do not carry the mechanical accompaniment.

There were times, out in the hay field, when I spent more time watching the swallows than watching where I was going. If I were raking, the windrows came out crooked as the swallows' flight, not the straight line my father insisted upon. So I'd have to do it over, but that was okay, too. It delayed the baling some more — mowing and raking were fun; baling was nothing but work — and gave me more time with the swallows.

It was always midsummer, too, when I found their unique mud-plastered nests under bridges or beneath the eaves of barn roofs and other sheds. They wait until there is an adequate supply of insect food nearby before nesting, which seems much more sensible than the tree swallows' hurry-up homemaking in April and early May.

Once, while hiking a gravel road past an abandoned farm, I saw barn swallows going in and out through a broken door on a large shed. I peeked in and saw an entire colony of the birds. There must have been 30 of the nests lined up almost side by side on the upper beams. Birds were whirling through the air like bees inside a hive. I dallied there for hours.

They are handsome birds, dressed in a blue-black tuxedo with a long, deeply forked tail, all set off by a rich orange throat

65

and that pale underside that constantly changes from white to cream to gold and back, depending on how the light strikes it.

And they may be the best fliers of any birds. Their streamlined body and that graceful tail enable them to pursue insects at breakneck speeds, abruptly changing directions without slowing. Acrobats on wings. If there really is such a thing as poetry in motion, it is the barn swallows, the birds of summer.

Only a matter of time

It's only a matter of time. So far, the hornets and I have avoided each other, but we're sure to meet one of these days.

Usually, by this time, I've discovered at least one huge hornet nest — and been stung a few times — while gathering raspberries. But most of the raspberry season is gone, and I've been able to pick more than a dozen quarts, and still no hornets.

I know they are nearby. I've seen a couple dallying near my peach tree, and one got inside the garage and was unable to get out. I think I even know where the nest is — somewhere inside that tangle of vines and brambles across the road — but so far, so good. However, there are still a few raspberries in that tangle, so I'm not getting too confident yet.

Actually, I get along very well with most bees and their relatives. Honey bees are always welcome, especially in early spring, when the fruit trees are in blossom. A colony of bumblebees has taken over an old birdhouse without incident, or our objections. Mud dauber wasps plaster their nests under the eaves nearly every year. And this summer we're even coexisting quite peacefully with the bizarre-looking green bees that have built an underground burrow beside our front door.

But these white-faced hornets (sometimes they're called bald-faced hornets, perhaps just to make them sound fiercer) are another matter. Oh, they're interesting enough. When the kids were small, I'd go out in October, after frost had shut down activity, and bring back one of the basketball-sized papier-mache nests. Then I'd slice the ingenious bag open and show the kids all the cells and compartments.

I still don't mind running across the nests in the fall, but in summer, I usually find them by accident, and that means a few painful stings. More often than not, the discovery is made by reaching down into a raspberry bush for some low-hanging fruit, and coming up with a hand on fire and swelling. Hornet stings hurt.

Occasionally, I see the nests before the hornets see me, and then I beat a strategic retreat, but this year the nests seem to be hidden better than ever. That means down lower in the briars and brambles, which, by the way, is supposed to mean a mild winter is in the offing. So maybe there is double good news from the hornets this year.

But I'm not counting on a sting-free year yet. Chances of getting through the rest of July and August without meeting the hornets are not good. Even though the raspberries are about finished, blueberries are still ahead, then the blackberries, and the elderberries.

It looks like the odds are still against me. It's only a matter of time.

Muskrats and moon shadows

The timing is ideal. The sun has just vanished below the hillside trees as we push off in the canoe, heading toward the western shore. The water has a golden glow from the sky's reflection, but already the shore is darkening rapidly, casting long shadows out over the pond.

Tree swallows are chasing each other, and kingbirds and thrashers are still jabbering away. A bullfrog in the weeds is bellowing at full blast, and far across the water another one answers. They sound like giants.

There is no wind at all; the water is smooth as glass. In the fading light, we can see hundreds of tiny insects whirling just inches above the water, frequently creating dimples in the surface as they touch down. Each time they hit the water, minute ripples appear, and each one is ringed in gold.

Fish are coming up for those insects, and their strikes punctuate the stillness. Are the insects mosquitoes? If so, we hope the fish eat them by the thousands. But mosquitoes aren't bothering us at all. They're the hunted instead of the hunters. That's fine with us.

A barely discernible, V-shaped ripple comes at us from shore. We stop paddling and watch. It's a muskrat — one of six we see on this jaunt — and it nearly collides with the canoe before realizing we're not a floating log. Then it frantically dives and retreats to the safety of the overhanging bushes.

The glow of leftover sunlight is gone, but now the nearly full moon is rising behind us — shaking loose from a gauzy veil of clouds — and the ripples are etched in silver instead of gold. A bat zig-zags by, just over our heads, and we hope it comes back so we can get a better look. The birds have fallen silent, but the bullfrogs are still at full volume, insects are droning from the woods and somewhere, far off in the distance, we hear an abrupt cry that momentarily chills the blood. Just one cry. An owl? It could be.

There are other sounds, too. Traffic on the spillway road is constant, and planes are heard frequently. There are the inevitable dogs barking, and we can even hear a party in progress on the far side of the pond. But none of that does much to disrupt the serenity of the night pond. If the muskrats and bullfrogs don't mind, why should we?

Lights are blinking on along the shore, and there seem to be far more homes than we ever noticed during the day. We can see a campfire on what we consider "our" island half a mile down the pond, and there's a fisherman's lantern glowing on the dam. Others are enjoying the night, too.

We keep relatively close to the shore, far enough out to avoid hitting rocks or brush, but near enough to hear and possibly see raccoons and other creatures venturing down the banks. We float much and paddle little, and what conversation there is consists of whispers. It's a place for the wildlings; we're merely spectators. We'd no more shout out there than we would yell during a symphony.

At the far end of the pond, we turn back. Now we can smell smoke from the island campfire, and we wish we had thought of camping there tonight. The fisherman at the dam has left. The party has moved indoors. Fewer dogs are barking. Fireflies are winking at us from the trees.

The stars are appearing rapidly; immediately Steve picks out the Big Dipper. The moon is straight ahead, so huge and yellow it looks unreal. Its reflection in the water is even larger, stretching out over nearly a mile of pond. It turns patches of lily pads and arrowhead plants into shimmering masses that appear metallic. We carefully paddle around the plants; it seems a crime to disturb such artistry.

We follow the eastern shore, where there are no cottages. Tall pines tower above us and now the long black shadows are created by moonglow. We float in and out of the shadows, and the breathtaking sight of the moon peeking through the pines reminds me of a similar scene I remember seeing somewhere. A painting? A photograph? Was it in some movie? Then it comes to me — it was in a TV commercial. How ironic, such a beautiful natural setting reminding me of television, which keeps most people from ever noticing the night sky.

There is a commotion in the weeds, and then all is silent once more. Perhaps a raccoon was after one of those frogs. May-

70

be a fox had come down that bank. Maybe it was another musk-rat. If we've seen half a dozen out on the pond, how many more are still in the shadows?

It's turning chilly, and we've been out for a couple of hours, so we aim for the cove where we began. Tomorrow, there will be fishermen and boaters all over the pond. They'll see the island and the pines and the lily pads. But they won't know the muskrats or the moon shadows or the bullfrogs or the intriguing colors. They won't know the pond at night. I'm glad we do.

A time to savor, a place to linger

July usually means a big drop in the music of the treetops. As the weather turns hot and summer settles in, the birds quiet down. Spring's serenades become a memory.

But there's still time to hear the songs — lots of them — if you're at the right place at the right time.

The right time is early morning and the right place — usually — is a meadow or clearing surrounded by woods. The deep woods itself is nearly silent now, save for the inevitable blue jays and an occasional tanager or vireo. You'll find plenty of chipmunks there, and mosquitoes, but not many birds.

Find a secluded meadow, however, one not marred by roadways or housing developments, and you'll still find plenty of activity in those magical hours just after daylight arrives, when heavy dew sparkles in the fresh sunshine, but before the heat becomes stifling.

Out in the open areas, where the waving grasses are waist-high, the meadowlarks and red-winged blackbirds are still nesting, and invasion brings a loud and spirited protest. Barn swallows are swooping low in headlong pursuit of insects, and marsh hawks are hovering overhead, poised for attack on unsuspecting mice.

Around the fringes, where taller bushes mix with saplings spreading out from the woods, brown thrashers, wrens, mockingbirds, catbirds, towhees and yellowthroats seem to be in competition, seeing which can drown out all the other voices. Thrashers ususally win — nothing is more irrepressible, not even the mockers.

At the very edge of the woods, in the tall trees, orioles continue to sing as if it were May — until perhaps 10 o'clock, depending on the temperature. Kingbirds make forays into the open, chasing insects, and cedar waxwings do the same. Doves are there, too, although less noisy.

The other day, we took a walk to such a clearing to check on a pair of bluebirds that had been up there earlier. Had they stayed for nesting? Would the rare but oh-so-delightful bluebirds be making a comeback?

We looked around for a couple of hours, and saw no bluebirds. But there were so many other birds for compensation that little time was wasted in mourning. And upon reflection, it's possible the bluebirds weren't seen simply because of all the distractions. It was a time to savor, a place to linger.

Just as good — for the birds — as the old meadow was a cut-over hillside that we've avoided the last two years since it was stripped by loggers. All that was left were several hundred stumps and a few dead, twisted trees not deemed worthy of cutting.

Now, though, there are thickets of scrub oaks that sprouted from the stumps, and acres of low-bush blueberries — ripe and scrumptious — and birds all over the place. Nearly every one of those stunted saplings rejected by the lumbermen serves as a singing perch all morning. The thrashers and mockingbirds appear to take turns up there, and orioles and red-wings jump in whenever there's a chance.

In a few weeks, even the meadows and new woodlots will become silent, but for now, in the cool morning hours, there is time to enjoy the songs one more time. Better not wait too long.

Summer place for a small boy

To a small boy — one away from street corners and video games and dirt bikes — a summer place is not a beach house or a cabin in New Hampshire. It's his own private little hideaway.

It can be a spare corner of the barn, or a tree house in the orchard, or maybe a lean-to back in the woods. It doesn't even have to be a shelter at all — perhaps just a secluded glen or a rugged ledge beside a stream. His summer place is any place where he has the privacy and time needed to nurture the adventures of fantasy.

There are few men who cannot remember such summer places. There is a foreverness to carefree boyhood summers; at least there was before television and organized activities took so much imagination out of childhood. Building a hut in the woods, or putting together a raft for the creek, or carving out a network of trails through a thicket occupied days and weeks. And years later, such projects are recalled with relish even though the hut leaked badly and the raft sank the first time it was launched.

In the woods, there are grape vines to swing on, like Tarzan, and mysterious paths to explore and animal tracks to investigate. For the imaginative, there are always outlaws to fight and grizzly bears to stalk and rattlesnakes to hunt. At the stream, there is gold to pan and waterwheels to build and alligators to battle.

Are such adventures passe? Do boys still take sticks into stands of ragweeds and pretend they're hacking their way through jungles with machetes? Do they still sneak up on a robin's nest and imagine they're trying to capture some rare and exotic eagle? Do they still dig into old cellar holes expecting to find buried treasure?

Those who don't are missing a special part of summer.

My brothers and I had new summer places each year, and we seldom left the farm. There was the year we built Tree Town — a series of planks linked a whole grove of saplings together, and we walked from one to another 10 feet above the ground. One year we set up camp in a ravine we called Beaver Valley, even though there were no beavers within miles, and spent weeks exploring and naming every knoll and ledge and brook. Another summer was spent converting an unused shed into a fort, and our imagination really ran wild the time we found an old spring wagon in a neighbor's shed; it quickly became a stagecoach in our minds.

Later, when the older boys had outgrown the fantasy world, I used as my summer place a huge, old mulberry tree. It hung out over a creek and I'd perch up there for hours, silently watching the muskrats and turtles and dragonflies in the water as well as the catbirds and thrashers and mockingbirds that came into the tree and gobbled the berries.

Eventually, of course, responsibilities beckoned me, too, and Tree Town and Beaver Valley and the mulberry tree had to be left behind. But they are still what I think of when I hear the term "summer place." I don't think that will ever change.

Too ornery to die out

It is mean and ugly and downright unsociable. It prefers to stay put, aloof and alone. But when it does decide to wander, all other creatures get out of its way.

Nobody wants to tangle with a snapping turtle.

The snapper is a reminder of the dinosaur era, the age of slow-moving, armor-plated reptiles and amphibians. It's been around for millions of years, and probably will be here for millions more. It just may be too ornery to die out.

Now, in mid-summer, the snapper is content to remain in the shallow streams and languid ponds and marshes. The male's battles have been fought. The female's eggs have been layed, buried and forgotten.

Unlike most pond turtles here, which are colorful and timid and do little besides sunning themselves on logs, the snapper is built for trouble. The shell is drab and rough with a hint of the spikes down the center like the old dinosaurs had. The claws are long and sharp. The head features a pair of fierce, unblinking eyes, like cold fireballs, and an even more intimidating hooked beak. A big snapper, and some here have shells 25 inches across, can actually take off a man's finger with that beak, so it's nothing to trifle with.

The snapper's disposition is just as ugly as its looks. When encountered, especially out of it's watery domain, the snapper is not reluctant at all about charging, whether it is meeting a raccoon or a dog or a man.

Man is the snapper's only real enemy. Sometimes, people being what they are, they'll kill snappers simply out of fear. Others may shoot a snapper just because it's there and some people have to kill.

But there are some who actually seek them out for their meat — they make great turtle soup. My father was in that group, and that's how I first met the snapper.

He and I had set out a dozen lines, baited with bits of chicken carcass — the smellier the better — in a small stream near our farm, and I ran ahead to check them the next morning. The first few were empty, but then I found one that I couldn't budge.

The line ran under a log at the shoreline, and I figured the hook had somehow gotten jammed into the bottom side of the log. So, I reached into the water to unhook it, and found myself grabbing a short, thick, writhing tail. I wasn't old enough, or smart enough, to let go, and I managed to pull that huge turtle out from under the log just as my father approached.

The pride in my accomplishment dimmed considerably when he asked what I would have done if I happened to grab the snapper's head, instead of its tail, down there in the muddy water. He said it wouldn't take me as long to count my fingers anymore.

I sometimes think of that first meeting when I come across a snapper, and I'm satisfied now to let it go its way while I go mine. I may not get much turtle soup these days, but at least I still have the same number of fingers on each hand.

It takes a genius

It would be so satisfying to be able to walk the fields and forests and reel off the names of all the insects we come across. Entomologists have my deepest respect — it takes a genius to remember all the thousands of species of bugs out there.

Summertime is butterfly time, and dragonfly time, and beetle time, and while it's easy enough to tell a butterfly from a beetle, correctly identifying each butterfly, each beetle, is another matter. Remembering them is no snap, either. I look up insects each year, and promptly forget most of them by the next summer.

Right now, the butterflies are abundant all over the meadows and pastures and stream sandbars. There are about 12,000 named species in this country, and many more awaiting classification. That's all. Each year I vow to learn a few more, and each year I find it more frustrating.

Knowing the monarchs is easy, and the cabbage butterflies are so common around my garden I know them only too well. I know the viceroys and the morning cloaks, and I even can tell some of the swallowtails apart. But that's about it.

The big clan of sulfur butterflies leaves me bewildered, as do the fritillaries. In fact, I have to look up that name every year. Checkerspots and painted ladies and white admirals have names more distinctive than they are, and there are dozens that are so drab I always dismiss them as moths.

Moths? That's another family so vast, and so difficult, I don't even try to sort them out. Except for the huge green luna moth, and the intriguing hummingbird moth, most are not special enough to warrant study.

Not when there are dragonflies around. Dragonflies and their cousins, the damselflies, are the big, helicopter-shaped insects of the watery places and open fields. They're no easier to identify than the butterflies. They're called skimmers and darners and several other names, but I usually have to consult the books to figure out which ones are bright green, which ones are blue, and which ones red. In fact, each summer I have a tough time remembering which are dragonflies and which are damselflies.

The beetles are too numerous for anybody to keep up with. There are 30,000 species in North America, but that's only a small part of their family. Across the world, there are 300,000 varieties.

Fireflies are beetles, and so are ladybugs and whirlygigs and June bugs and tumblebugs and all sorts of borers and carrion insects. And everyone who has a garden knows the Japanese beetle and Colorado potato beetle far too well.

My favorite beetle, though, is something called a click beetle. Most of the time, it's an inconspicuous little bug that favors decaying wood. But then it goes into its act. When overturned, it can flip high in the air, often landing upright. The "click" name comes from the sharp sound it makes when it launches itself upward.

The insect season is just warming up. August soon will be bringing many more species for us. That's when the grasshoppers and crickets, the cicadas and katydids, are in their prime.

The parade won't slow down until first frost. By then the monarch butterflies will be heading south. The crickets will be trying to get into houses. The fireflies will have vanished.

And people like me still will be trying to figure out which is the sulphur butterfly and which is the fritillary.

Lilies' day in the sun

Think about it — how many orange wildflowers do you know? Lots of white ones and yellow ones. Plenty of blue flowers and red flowers. Even some purple and some pink.

But orange? Very few.

Except for the wild lilies.

This is their time; this is the time for orange in the overgrown meadows and weedy bottomlands and uncut roadsides.

It's the height of summer, and that phrase can refer to the size of weeds and flowers as well as to the temperature. Any sunny place that escapes mowing is jammed right now with flowering plants, all stretching toward the sky.

They are so much bigger and tougher by necessity than the dainty flowers of spring — the violets and marsh marigolds and bluets. Such plants could not survive now; they'd be crowded out by the towering plants now in their prime. The spring flowers would never feel the sunshine.

Most summer "flowers" are considered weeds, and many are too common to really be appreciated, but an unbiased observer must admit there is no finer blue than that of the chicory, or a deeper, richer gold than that of the black-eyed Susan. Thick stands of Queen Anne's lace — white as snow — or the right yellow goldenrods that will be coming later certainly would qualify as flowers if they weren't so abundant.

That's the way it is with the lilies. They are special, or should be, because they are such a unique color. Except for the jewel weeds — which some people call touch-me-nots — there aren't many other orange flowers around. And the lilies surely are much prettier than jewel weeds.

Yes, the lilies can be "weeds" too. Once established, they spread quickly and are exceedingly difficult to grub out. They're as tough as chicory, as persistent as goldenrods. But, fortunately, they usually choose places not used much by gardeners or farmers or lawn purists.

Of the numerous wild lilies in this area, the Turk's cap is the tallest, the most colorful and has the most imaginative name. Among its relatives are the day lily, the tiger lily, the Canada lily, the Michigan lily and the wood lily. All are tall, angular plants and most have similar blossoms — nodding flowers with long, narrow petals that sweep backward. Most are spotted, including the tiger lily, and what tiger has spots instead of stripes?

The Turk's cap variety has perhaps the longest petals, and they sweep back the most, and do, I supposed, resemble a Turk's cap. Frequently, they'll grow to eight feet, and the color is as orange as an October sunset. Sometimes it's so bright that it's nearly red.

At the height of summer, the liles are just coming into their prime. If midsummer really is the crowning glory of the year, maybe the wild lilies deserve some recognition as the gems in that crown. One thing is certain — summer would be far less colorful without them.

The pole light

It took a long time for me to put my finger on it, but I knew there was something wrong with my house. Now I realize what's missing — there is no pole light.

Pole lights, the outdoor kind, used to be very important to me, particularly in mid-summer and mid-winter, and I'm amazed I went this long without figuring out what was wrong here. Apparently, I've slipped into the curse of suburban living — looking inward instead of outward.

Out on the farm, the pole light was meant to provide security and safety. To me, it also provided a means of observing the backyard ecosystem. In other words, via that light, I could spy on the beasts and bugs of the night and, in winter, tune in on the developing weather patterns.

Our light was attached to the top of the woodshed, about 20 feet behind the house. That was just the right distance for checking on the snow. We'd flip the light on, and any flakes drifting past it would be instantly dramatized by the light beam and the black background. Then Mom would push up the heat a bit.

It was also perfect for exposing the raccoons and foxes that sneaked into the yard, bent on raiding the cats' dishes or invading the chicken coop. I'd sit motionless at the window until I detected a sound or movement outside, and then I'd hit the switch.

But at this time of year, the light served another purpose, highly important to my brothers and me. It drew moths. That was a great summer night activity, before TV drew people into living rooms at sunset. There seemed to be a lot more moths in those days, too, but that could be just time's distortion of memory.

We'd sit there as expectant as kids waiting for Red Sox players outside Fenway Park, ticking off the names of each new arrival. There are the millers! Look at that sphinx! Isn't that luna something! Hey, there's the isabella, the one that comes from the woollybear caterpillar!

The light mesmerized the moths, and the moths mesmerized us.

Occasionally, we'd even see a cecropia moth, although in those days we called them silk moths. They're huge, as big as some songbirds, and seeing one would highlight our vigil. After watching a cecropia for a few minutes, any other sighting would be anticlimactic, so we'd head for bed.

I don't think I've taken a good look at a cecropia or luna moth since I moved here. There are still lights, of course, but they're over doors (too near the house) or out on the street (too high) to get the same effect.

No, it's just not the same without my pole light. And I miss it. I wonder if there's room in the backyard for a woodshed.

Easy pickings

Our frantic harvesting of the wild summer fruit is starting to wind down now, but there is one major project left. However, that one — picking elderberries — will be a breeze. It always is.

Elderberries are so easy to gather it is like taking cans off the supermarket shelf, except that they are fresh and free. It's a wonder, and a shame, there are so few people picking them these days.

After sloshing around in marshes and battling mosquitoes in pursuit of blueberries, and getting scratched and stabbed repeatedly going after raspberries and blackberries, taking the elderberries is no trouble at all.

They often grow in the lowlands, to be sure, but almost as many bushes are along country roads, scattered around meadows and even up on hillsides. They have no vines, no thorns, and do not guard their fruit in any way. It's just hanging there, waiting to be taken.

Best of all, elderberries can be picked in clusters, just as they grow. The juicy fruit is tiny, and it would take forever to fill a bucket if they had to be picked individually, the way most other wild berries are picked, but one snap of the cluster stem is all it takes to gather a couple of hundred berries. At that rate, the buckets fill quickly.

Often just one bush will yield enough fruit to satisfy a picker. It seems there has never been a bad year for elderberries. The bushes are always laden with the purple-black clusters, weighing down the branches almost to the point of breaking them. They blossom late, well into June, when their white flowers highlight the country roadsides, so they are never curtailed by late frosts.

Nor are they curtailed by anything else. Elderberry bushes are tough, too tough sometimes for farmers and gardeners who try to get rid of unwanted bushes. They just keep coming up when chopped off, and new bushes spring up every spring from seeds scattered by birds in August.

There was a time when elderberries were sought eagerly every summer. Elderberry pie was considered a delicacy, and I guess it still is in some places. And then there was the elderberry wine that was made on every farm for those times in winter when a man gets to feeling "puny."

We don't make much wine, and elderberry pie doesn't measure up to the blueberry and raspberry pies, but we turn out jar after jar of jelly. It tastes mighty good in the middle of winter when the snow is flying. It would be a crime to let the elderberries go to waste, especially when filling the buckets is so easy.

Thunderstorms

Thunderstorms fascinate me. Always have. Especially those that sneak up on us late at night, then erupt like a volcano.

I know sky-ripping lightning and ground-shaking thunder terrify some people, but even while they are terrifying, they're also awesome and intriguing. They show the violent might sometimes found in nature. Nobody who respects nature ever says it is all sunshine and butterflies.

It seems to take the late-night solitude and darkness to do the thunderstorms justice. At that hour, with the blackness of the universe for a backdrop and the suddenness that belongs only to something that approaches while the world sleeps, it becomes a phenomenon of another dimension. It can be eerie, unreal, like some scene out of a dream. Especially when the storm wakes you from a deep sleep.

For the storm's duration, nothing else exists, at least nothing that can compete with that unleased fury.

I remember a storm of years ago, when I was a boy on a farm in Ohio. The jarring thunder practically shook me right out of bed, and when the rain started pattering on the tin roof of the porch outside my window, I gave up trying to sleep.

As I watched at the window, the booming thunder continued to build, as if explosions were feeding upon explosions, the crackling, flashing lightning began streaking through the blackness, momentarily bathing the countryside in a brilliant yellow glow.

I could see across the fields to the church steeple in town, two miles away. Even at midday, in summer, it was seldom that visible because of the dust of the fields. Then it would be total darkness again. Seconds later, I could see the thick grove of trees surrounding my grandmother's house. Then, back to blackness.

At the height of the storm, just as I was wondering how my brothers could sleep with that incredible din going on above, a jagged arm of lightning darted down and struck a huge apple tree in our orchard, perhaps 200 feet from where I sat. I was spellbound.

That tree had always seemed the strongest, most solid thing in the world to me. Its trunk was more than four feet thick, its branches curving upward as if supporting the entire sky. To a small boy, it did. I would climb as high as I could and imagine myself as the lookout on a pirate ship, the waving wheat fields beyond the orchard my golden ocean of limitless horizons.

The lightning bolt split that tree in two, slicing it right down the center, all the way to the ground.

I loved that tree, but instead of resenting the storm, I was captivated by its awesome power. I've been a thunderstorm watcher ever since.

Now I know some of the scientific explanations of lightning and thunder, but science doesn't really come into play when these storms hit in the dead of night. They are too loud, too bright, too wild, too unpredictable, too spectacular for science.

Let others try to cope with them as best they can, whether it be by ignoring them or hiding under the bed. I know where I'll be — right there at the window.

So good for the ego

Every gardener should grow sunflowers once in a while, even if he's not interested in collecting the seeds. They're colorful, easy to grow, and so good for the ego.

Too often, weekend gardeners out here in suburbia find themselves with spindly tomato plants that aren't strong enough to hold themselves up, much less the tomatoes; sweet corn that gets knee-high by the Fourth of July, and stays there, and cabbages that would make a sauerkraut-maker burst out laughing — or crying.

And this is after all the careful planning and plowing and planting, the bags of fertilizer, the compost and mulch, the weeding and watering. Eventually, though, the weeds grow as if by magic; the vegetables become anemic.

Part of the problem, of course, is that even those with the best of intentions, those who rejoice over the first radish of spring, have a tendency to lose some of that enthusiasm when Saturday afternoons reach 95 degrees and there are fishing and golf and tennis beckoning. So the garden is neglected and the soil dries up and growth is stymied. And by the end of the summer, the gardener surveys it all and wonders where he went wrong.

But a few hills of sunflowers can bring back the confidence. It's pretty hard not to grow tall sunflowers.

I say I grow them for the huge seed heads, so that I won't have to buy so many when winter bird-feeding begins. But I actually harvest only a few of the seeds. Chickadees, house finches, blue jays and other birds beat me to them. Sure, I could put a bag over the top as some people do, but then I'd miss the acrobatic shows the birds put on as they try to pluck the seeds from the upside-down heads.

And even when I do cut a head and store it away in the shed or garage, it seems the chipmunks and mice usually help themselves. Once, I remember, a chipmunk stole every seed from three huge heads and transported the entire cargo to his burrow beneath the shed. I dug up the tunnel and found the cache, but then decided he had worked hard enough for his winter store and let him keep the loot.

Right now, I don't even think about whether I'll get the seeds this year or not. Those heads are bright yellow flowers atop stalks seven feet tall, dwarfing the rest of the garden plants. So what if the tomatoes are a disaster and the pole beans even worse? The sunflowers are gigantic; they couldn't be better. They make me feel like a successful, green-thumb gardener.

And my conscience about neglecting the rest of the vegetables is soothed once more. That's reason enough to keep planting sunflowers.

Old boats and dignity

Once, it was shiny and new. Now, it is a rotting wreck. It had been a valued possession, perhaps even an indispensible piece of equipment. Now, it is forgotten, cast aside without a second thought.

There are so many of them — old wooden boats, I mean — and I can't understand it. How can anybody simply throw an old boat away?

Undoubtedly, it is because of my inland, cornfield-country heritage, but I've always had this special feeling for boats. Where I grew up, boats of any kind, even rowboats, were not taken for granted, as they are here. In New England boats seem to be as much a part of life as tractors are to midwesterners.

Perhaps, then, my attitude toward boats may be considered sentimental, or worse, but to me a boat has a personality, an understanding. Again, I'm talking specifically about the small wooden rowboats, skiffs and canoes. Newer fiberglass and aluminum models strike me as much colder and impersonal, and I have no feelings at all for the yachts and sailboats and inboards and all the other pleasure craft on the water.

But the old rowboat is something else. It is a companion and partner of the man pulling on the oars; not a slave, not a toy. It is a thing to be cared for as one would care for a faithful dog. It does its best work when treated with kindness and respect. When its days of activity are over, it should be allowed to fade away with some dignity.

That's not the way it is, however.

In a river near my home, I know of four skeletons of rowboats lying in uneasy repose at the shoreline — and skeletons they are, for there is little left other that the splintered shells and wooden ribs. Most of the side planking is gone, and on each of the four boats, either the bow or the stern is missing.

Two of the boats are almost completely buried in the mud. Another is lying upside down in tall weeds on a sand bar. The fourth is jammed between two trees, along with a mass of driftwood and debris, about 20 feet from the river, evidently deposited there by some floodwaters. All are a mile or more from the nearest house.

It seems I run across similar skeletons along any waterway here, whether inland or saltwater, and I wonder why. Were the boats discarded because they were wrecked, or did they become such forlorn shambles only after they were abandoned?

Who knows or cares? Nobody, I guess. Perhaps it's not important, at least not more important than why old cars are left to rust away in many of the southern and midwestern woods.

Except that these are boats, and boats are still something special to me. I haven't been away from the flatlands long enough to lose that feeling yet. Maybe I will some day, but not yet.

Dawn on the beach

It's 6 a.m. and the beach is nearly deserted. Just the way I like it. One man walking his dog. One jogger. Hundreds of birds. And me.

In a few hours, the sand will be jammed with sunbathers and blankets and radios. Lots of noise.

But at 6 a.m., it's a place of tranquility. It is not silent — not by a long shot — with the roiling, crashing surf and screaming gulls, but the sounds fit in just right. They are altogether appropriate.

There is a satisfying might to the sea that both inspires and soothes. Timeless. Untamed. Powerful.

Beaches are not my usual habitat; I'm more at home in the fields and forests. But I'm pulled to the sea a few times each year — more often in winter than summer — and perhaps it is the infrequency of my visits that keep them refreshing and enlightening.

It's hazy this morning, and the sun is a pale yellow as it struggles to burn through the curtain of mist. The waves, though, are white-capped and furious, charging in and slamming into the breakwater rocks. Again and again and again.

Gulls, the ever-present gulls, dominate the scene as always. Wheeling and circling over the surf. Poking around in the sand. Lined up on the rocks. Herring gulls and black-backed gulls and Bonaparte's gulls and probably a few others.

Mixed in with the gulls, and far more attractive, are dozens of graceful terns. They swoop and hover and fly rings around the gulls. Right now, the terns are the stars of the show. By afternoon, when the beach is crowded with people, the terns will be out of sight.

Little flocks of sandpipers hurry along the shore, flying about like so many wind-tossed leaves. They turn and fly and alight together, all for one and one for all. A swirling cloud of feathers and wings.

In a tiny inlet, where the sea deposited its weeds and refuse

95

during the night, the birds are as thick and industrious as chickens in a barnyard. Sandpipers of several sizes, shapes and species. Plovers. Dunlins. Turnstones.

The ruddy turnstones, in particular, are fascinating. With their golden-brown backs and black chins and chests, they remind me of quail as they nervously scurry around, pecking and probing every bit of seaweed. That's my farmland heritage showing through, I know, but nearly every bird I see at the beach corresponds to inland creatures.

Just offshore, a flock of eight cormorants floats easily in the churning swells. They disappear from view every few seconds, but bob up in the next instant, completely at ease even though tossed about like corks. They're as calm as mallards on a farm pond. The sea is their own.

Perhaps it is the waves, and the vastness of the sea itself, that demand the most attention, at least for landlubbers like me. That vastness is almost beyond my comprehension. A sailboat on the horizon is about the limit of my understanding.

I stand and look and listen to the sea, and marvel. Somewhere, thousands of miles away, those waves, that tide, is lapping up against another shore. Another continent. Another culture.

And right now, there's probably another man standing there and enjoying it all. The terns. The surf. The sounds. He may even be another landlubber.

Summer rain

Rain patters on the leaves, now slick and shiny as if varnished. The ground squishes underfoot, tiny pools forming around my boots as each step is taken.

The wind twists and shifts, often sending the drizzle into my face. I pull my hat lower, hunch down deeper into my jacket, and try again to turn away from the cold spray. But I keep walking.

Walking in the rain — and watching and listening — holds a fascination for me. Just as a snowstorm lures me to the woods in winter to contemplate its serenity and beauty, so a summer rain pulls me out there for . . . what? It's hard to say. Something.

The woods are less active during rain, of course. Not as many birds are chirping. Fewer squirrels and chipmunks are scurrying about. You'll even find fewer spiders and ants. But there are compensations — fewer mosquitoes, too.

Really, though, maybe I walk the woods in the rain to feel, rather than see. Maybe it's the primal wildness a drenching rain brings to the woods. Maybe it's the scrubbed look. Maybe it's the sparkling beads of water on each leaf. Maybe it's the freshness of the mosses, which are instantly revived by each rain. There's nothing greener than mosses in the rain; they soak it up like sponges.

Sure, walking in the rain, especially in the woods, gets you soaked. Every time you brush a branch, you get a shower. After 10 seconds, the bushes and tall grasses are wet enough to drench your legs. But as a wise philosopher once told me — actually, it was Steve when he was 14 — "It's better to be a lot wet than a little wet."

What he meant, of course, was that most people try so hard to keep from getting wet they can't appreciate rain. But once you are soaked to the skin, you have no reason to hurry any more, and you can start enjoying it.

Occasionally, rain walkers find something special. Once, I came upon a fawn, stumbling about on uncertain legs. I remember finding an owl huddled on a pine limb, patiently waiting out the rain while trying to sleep. Another time, I saw a skink — a type of lizard — with a bright blue tail, running along the top of a fence. And there was the perky little yellowthroat singing away in a downpour as if it were a sunny morning in May.

But such sightings are the exceptions. Usually, the featured attractions are far more subtle . . . runoff water shoving decaying leaves aside as it creates instant brooks on the hillsides . . . the dimpled surface of the pond in the hollow . . .the glistening sheen on the eons-old rocks, momentarily renewed by the washing. Such things need to be felt, not just seen.

So I walk in the rain. And I no longer care how it looks to others, not since adopting another motto — this one came from somebody's grandfather — "If you never do what other men call foolish, you'll only know what foolish men know."

Looking out the top

Maples may be best. Oaks and beeches are fine, too, although they usually have too few limbs near the ground. My personal favorite was the sycamore, but that was in another part of the country. There aren't enough sycamores around here.

The subject is tree-climbing, something country kids usually revert to at this time of summer, when the season is growing a little tattered around the edges. Swimming seldom loses its attraction, but many other summer activities — baseball, biking, even fishing — seem to take too much effort for these dog days. But climbing trees is just about right for late August.

As a parent, I'm a little apprehensive when the kids climb trees. There is always a chance of injury, of course. But as long as they are careful, I usually don't stop them. I remember too well all the trees I climbed.

In fact, I probably thought trees were put on earth just for little boys — and girls — to climb. I began with the old apple trees in our orchard — out of Mom's sight — and eventually graduated to the towering oaks, maples and those majestic sycamores in Gib's Woods.

It was another world up there. I still remember the pulsating tension that built up as I forced myself to go higher and higher, limb by limb. I never really conquered my fear of those dizzy heights, particularly when the branches swayed in the wind, but the stomach-tightening, heart-pounding fear only made the climb more attractive, more adventurous. When I came down, I felt immensely proud of my feat, and of myself. Even on the ground, I felt I was floating on the clouds.

The smaller the child, of course, the higher those trees appear. Those 20-foot apple trees that I first climbed seemed as high as the sky. I couldn't believe it years later when I returned and looked at those gnarled old trees. Could I really have trembled with excitement upon finally reaching the top of such insignificant trees?

Memories of childhood adventures tend to distort facts anyway, and when they involve objects seen through young eyes and confronted by small bodies, those objects grow to awesome dimensions. It was a major test in our group to "look out the top" of the apple trees. Once you did that, once you poked your head above the highest branch, you belonged. After that, any challenge to your courage was easier to meet.

Hours flew by in the apple trees. We spied on imaginary armies from the upper branches. We scanned the seas for islands to discover. We fought off raging tigers. And we ate an awful lot of green apples.

In Gib's Woods, we climbed to birds' nests and tentatively reached into hollow limbs that we hoped held baby squirrels. Or we just climbed to see how high we could go and how far we could see. It was daring, and scary, and perhaps just a bit foolish, but it was fun.

Climbing trees opens new horizons, both literally and figuratively. You can see over fences and across fields and into the next block. But more than that, the tree-climber can see inside himself. He'll have faced a giant obstacle — fear — and overcome it. And he'll have soared to incredible personal heights, even if he is only 20 feet off the ground.

Green heron time

It isn't hard to tell the days are already getting shorter. All I have to do is clock the green heron's arrival at the marsh each evening.

Herons are strange-looking birds, and the green heron is perhaps the strangest of the clan, but he can tell time. When he sails in on his hump-backed, awkward flight, I know it will be dark in an hour. He's always on schedule.

The heron didn't nest in the marsh and made only occasional appearances there earlier in the summer, but he practically has the place all to himself in late August and he knows it. He's the whole show.

In spring, the marsh is noisy with the spring peepers chanting and the red-winged blackbirds squabbling and the kingfisher rattling incessantly. When the heron stopped by then, he was lost in the crowd, and quickly moved on.

In summer, the peepers piped down and the red-wings settled into a less vociferous mood, but then the bullfrogs were booming out through the nights and the kingbirds and swallows and mosquitoes kept the place alive, if not by sound, then by action.

Now, though, most of the kingbirds and swallows are gone, the red-wings are somberly awaiting departure, and the frogs are content to spend their remaining weeks of activity in silence.

There are plenty of insects still around — water striders and whirligig beetles and dragonflies, as well as mosquitoes — but they belong in the background, not on center stage.

So the green heron takes charge. He arrives an hour before dark and promptly lets all the marsh creatures know he's there by perching halfway up a dead maple and squawking loudly for 15 or 20 minutes. If there is a reason for the calling, other than sheer exuberance, it isn't evident.

Then he goes to work, prowling the shoreline in search of whatever happens by, minnows, water insects, crustaceans, even frogs and snakes. He's sharp-eyed and quick, thrusting his long beak into the water in a flash and usually coming back up with his prey snared.

The green heron is something of a stepchild of the heron family. Not only is he chunky and big-headed in contrast to the angular, almost graceful form of his cousins, but he is tagged with an inaccurate name. He's not green at all, but blue-gray across the back and shoulders, with a reddish neck and streaked head.

But they couldn't call him a blue heron, because there already were great blue and little blue herons. So the little misfit was labeled a green heron. Maybe that's why he makes such a fuss in the marsh now. It's his one chance to be the star of the show, and he wants to make the most of it.

It's later than you think

It may be hard to believe right now, but within six weeks we'll have the first frost of fall. That's what the katydids are saying.

The nighttime insect chorus has reached full volume, and that means the katydids have, too. They're among the last of the night criers to join in, and according to folklore, when the katydids start screeching, you can figure on frost in six weeks.

Let's see now. Six weeks will take us into October. Yes, we could have frost by early October. There are years when frost doesn't hit until a few weeks later, but usually the katydids are pretty close. Within two weeks, or so.

These are the noisiest nights of the year. For several weeks — as the humidity and heat climbed — the insect chant has been increasing. There are cicadas and crickets and certain kinds of grasshoppers, and now katydids, all joining in what some naturalist once called "the wackiest orchestra on earth."

It's difficult, however, for even a naturalist to call this racket of the darkness a song. It's a constant din of buzzing, humming, scratching, creaking and clicking. Somehow, it all blends together and it's tough for most of us to pick out the various insects, but obviously they have little trouble separating the "voices" themselves — this is their courtship time.

Unlike birds, most of which attract mates with melodic songs, the insects have to resort to all sorts of unique forms of making noise. Some rub their wings together. Several species use one wing as a fiddle bow, drawing it across the other. And some forms of grasshoppers "sing" by standing on their front legs and rubbing their back legs across small, stiff pegs on their wings.

Now, with the green, long-antennaed katydids adding their monotonous, three-note tunes, the chorus has reached full membership. Just step outside on some hot, humid night, and listen. The sound from the trees and bushes and meadow grasses is almost a roar. The height of summer is also a climax for the insect season. Soon it will be September, with its cooler — and quieter

103

— nights. It won't be entirely silent until heavy frosts arrive, of course — whether that comes in six weeks or not — but there will be a gradual thinning of the night criers as autumn nears.

Perhaps the katydid is no better at predicting the seasonal changes than the woodchuck, which supposedly also can see six weeks ahead in February, but its mere arrival can bring on thoughts of fall's approach.

The katydids are saying that summer is passing quickly, and now it's a downhill stroll into autumn. They say it's time to think about gathering firewood and cleaning out the garden and maybe trying to get in one last weekend at the beach.

Daytime temperatures may say it's still summer. But the nights, and the katydids, say it's later than you think.

September song

September is on the horizon; September and all that it means. It's the season of change, the transformation of summer into autumn.

September is a refreshing breeze that stirs the soul, and makes the feet yearn to be out roaming again. It's a mood that rekindles ambition, whets the appetite for adventure and somehow reminds men of forgotten ties with the past. That feeling, that call of the wild, may be the biggest reason why men still hunt each fall.

September is a restlessness among the birds, too, particularly in the evenings. Wandering flocks of robins and flickers and red-wings ride the breezes seemingly nervous in anticipation of the silent signal for migration, still weeks away. They hurry from meadow to woods to pasture, with no more a goal in mind than the wind-tossed leaves.

September is scarlet flames on the sumac leaves and first hint of orange in the maples. By the month's end, the sumac will be in full warpaint, and the maples will be ablaze, their fiery colors leaping from tree to tree and turning entire hillsides into postcard scenes of dazzling color.

September is ripening apples and withering roses, grapes hanging heavy on the vines and tomatoes well past their prime. It's a time for harvesting the fruits of autumn, and bidding farewell to the bounty of summer.

September is deep blue, smog-free skies, and the first whiff of wood smoke from fireplace chimneys. The first fire, usually lit before storm windows are in place or blankets brought out of closets, triggers another autumn sound, the roar of chainsaws in the woods.

September is kids trudging off to school, dreading the homework but secretly glad to be back with their friends. It is lively Saturdays on the football and soccer fields, and weeds growing unchallenged on the baseball diamonds. It is closing the summer cottage and make plans to store the motorboat and one last picnic at the beach.

September is the fox yipping in the moonlight, and a hundred dogs, perhaps hearing the same ancestral call, quivering and tugging at leashes and gazing at distant forests. They want, and need, to be out running free, as free as their wild cousins, as free as that tantalizing breeze.

September is heavy dew at dawn, fog in the hollows at dusk, and frequently mid-day heat that makes you think July has returned. Evening comes slightly earlier each night, and morning loses a few minutes as well. Shortly after mid-month, the hours of darkness will outnumber hours of daylight, and the clock of the seasons will click past another celestial milestone.

September is squirrels and chipmunks frantically searching for acorns and nuts, sounding as large as bears as they scurry about in the fallen leaves. There are goldfinches collecting thistledown now and nighthawks soaring overhead at dusk and half-grown rabbits loping about on hind legs that are far too long for them.

September is cleanup time in the garden, digging up the last carrots and potatoes, collecting the remaining pumpkins and squashes and cucumbers, and pulling up the withered vines. And, in a sense, when you put away the hoe and wheelbarrow and watering can, and all the other tools of the garden, you also are putting away summer itself.

For September is also the awaiting of the first frost, which one night will creep down from the hills and make the season change official. It won't happen this week, or next, but it's coming.

Fall fever

The cool weather of recent days had more to do with it than flipping the calendar page from August to September, but that delightful feeling — fall fever — has struck again.

Others may mourn the passing of summer, and think of autumn's arrival as nothing more than the return of heating bills and school chores, but it doesn't have to be that way. September can mean a new, invigorating sense of wonder. To those in tune with the countryside, it brings an eagerness to be out and about again, a restlessness of the spirit.

Fall fever strikes those who prefer stirring breezes to listless summer heat, those who would rather climb ledges than lie on beaches, those who enjoy the satisfaction of completed cycles as much as the urgency of birth and growth.

That restlessness, that irresistible urge to be out and roaming, is perhaps the strongest lure of the season. For centuries, wanderers — nomads, explorers, migrant workers — have felt that call early each autumn and responded. The breezes sang of new adventures, new hopes, and they just had to move on. Over the next hill. Across the prairie. Beyond the mountains. Down the rivers.

Much of our own west would not have been explored nearly as early, or as eagerly, had it not been for fall fever. The fur trappers and hunters of years ago often told how they wearied of their tasks by February and March each winter and longed to return to civilization. But when autumn arrived, the fever hit them all over again, and they had to answer the call. They just had to.

It is not that much different now. We may not wander off into the mountains for months on end, but just check the traffic out beyond the suburbs on crisp Sunday afternoons in September and October, and you'll see that restlessness is still with us. Maybe they're heading for apple orchards or antique stores or flea markets or just out to see the foliage, but whatever the reason, people have to be out and moving. Fall fever.

You can see it in the animals and birds, too. Dogs that have never hunted strain at their leashes and gaze longingly at distant hills. Foxes bark at the moon. Raccoons and deer dally at their feeding until after dawn. Skunks and opossums wander in the darkness, and many die beneath our wheels. Chipmunks, gathering acorns and nuts, chatter in sheer ecstasy.

Already, among the birds, early migrants are flocking and riding the breezes across the meadows, streams and woods. Cedar waxwings and swallows soar and dive over the water. Red-winged blackbirds whirl about in the evenings and, just before dusk, flocks of nighthawks swoop out of the sky.

All will be leaving when the weather turns colder, but that is weeks away yet. For now, they are enjoying their most carefree season. The nesting is finished; the fledglings are grown. There is still plenty of food — insects, seeds, berries — and the living is easy. But they cannot relax; they, too, have been inflicted with fall fever.

There are not many better feelings.

Just one robin

It was only one robin. I shouldn't have gotten so upset about it. Who's going to notice one less robin in the world?

But I did get upset, and I'm still upset. Why did they have to shoot a robin? Why is the urge to kill something — anything — so strong in some people?

I had met the two young men high on a hill, far back in the woods. They were carrying rifles, slung carelessly over their arms. I suppose they were looking for squirrels, but I'm not sure, and I didn't wait around to find out.

My dog was up there with me, and I've seen enough "hunters" who shoot anything that moves to realize Rusty was in danger. So I called loudly to him, and hurried down the hill before either of us was mistaken for a squirrel.

Hours later, I returned to the foot of the hill to help my sons, who were collecting beer cans and bottles for an ecology project. The men with rifles were still there, firing round after round at bottles set upon rocks.

Evidently, the hunting had not been good, so they were taking out their frustration on the bottles, and leaving broken glass scattered all over the picturesque hillside.

They left shortly after we arrived, and that's when one of my boys found the robin. He called me over, and asked why the robin had died. I told him it was shot, probably by the two men we had just seen, and again he asked why.

I couldn't answer that one. There were no answers; none that made sense.

But it was just one robin, wasn't it?

Just one songbird. Just one of the birds we so anxiously await each spring. Just one of the hundreds that strut about the lawn and meadows and pastures all summer. Just another bird that sings before daybreak and nests in the backyard maple and raids our strawberry patch.

Just a robin.

I wondered how much satisfaction those men got from

shooting down a bird that usually is as fearless, as tame, as a barnyard chicken. The flock I had seen on the hillside earlier that day seemed reluctant to fly at all. They were huddled in a cedar thicket, perhaps resting up for the long flight south.

I wondered how many other birds — woodpeckers or chickadees or mockingbirds — also were lying dead back in the woods. If the men shot a robin, why wouldn't they shoot the other birds, too?

Why not — there were no squirrels to shoot that day.

I wondered if my sons, Steve and Scott, understood just what happened. Bettie and I had tried to teach them to respect and appreciate all wild creatures. Would they feel a twinge of regret, or anger, over the robin's death.

Would they accept it as the way some people are?

Or would they not care at all?

After all, it was only one robin.

Monarchs are marking time

They're facing a long, incredible migration, but right now they're the picture of contentment. For the monarch butterflies, early autumn is the season of plenty.

In a few weeks, when frost starts stealing down from the north, the orange and black monarchs will gather for their arduous flights to Florida — the most remarkable journey of any of our insects. The seemingly fragile butterflies will follow the coastline, contending with storms and winds and a hundred other obstacles on their way to winter grounds. Other insects — even other butterflies — stay here, preferring to spend the winter in dormant stages, but for some reason the monarchs are programmed to fly thousands of miles.

At times, they travel in flocks that look like orange clouds. Often they string out in wavering lines that stretch for miles. When they roost for the night, they can cover trees and bushes with thick blankets of wings the color of October sunsets.

Nature has given them one break; evidently they don't taste very good. Birds pass them up. There is no other way they could migrate along the same routes as birds and survive. In fact, their taste is so bad that birds won't even attack viceroy butterflies because they resemble the monarchs.

Not all the monarchs will survive the round trip, of course. Many of them — particularly the males — will succumb on the way. Enough females will make it, though. They'll find their way back here, lay their eggs in milkweed plants and complete their cycle before dying.

But those migratory flights are a few weeks off yet. For now, the butterflies are enjoying themselves in the tall meadows and pastures. They are bouncing from asters to joe-pye weeds to goldenrods to the dozens of other wildflowers now in full maturity. They flit about aimlessly, as carefree as the breeze itself.

You'll find them most active when the meadows are in full sunlight. They need that warmth. When evening falls, and the temperature dips, the monarchs grow sluggish. They cannot compete with cold. They'll cling to branches or bushes until the sunshine returns with its reviving rays. Then, when they receive the signal that a killing frost is imminent, they'll flutter off toward the southland.

Scientists have watched the monarchs' migration for years — it even took them decades to locate the winter quarters of the western monarchs in Mexico — but nobody has yet determined just why they make such journeys. Nor can they explain how the butterflies can find their way over such long distances. Or how they can be blown far off course, often well out over the ocean, and still have the strength in those delicate wings to reach their destinations.

But they make it. Somehow.

For now, though, they are marking time. Autumn may mean an end to life cycles for most northern insects, but for the monarch butterflies, it's more of a beginning. The critical stages of their lives are just ahead.

The dog, the hawk and I

According to the calendar, autumn begins on Sept. 23, but that's not really true. We know better — the dog, the hawk and I.

Fall has already begun.

It began several days ago, on a brilliant afternoon when sparkling sunshine and tugging breezes combined for an irresistible lure. As they so often do, they pulled me out of the house, beyond the backyard, up through the woods to the top of the hill.

Rusty, who seemingly lives for such wandering, went along. While I walked the long, winding path, Rusty roamed on all sides, trotting, stopping, loping, sniffing, running, stopping again. And he still beat me to the top.

That's where we found the hawk, and that's where we found autumn.

There were few signs along the way that we were stepping into another season. A couple of young maples near the river showed hints of pink and yellow in their leaves, and Rusty chased two squirrels that had ventured to the ground to collect fallen acorns.

But for the most part, the woods and hillside looked summer-sleepy yet. The canopy above was solid green, and the ground below was somber and silent. No piles of fallen leaves yet. No rustle that makes a tiny chipmunk sound as large as a deer.

Halfway up, we flushed a pair of grouse, the "partridges" so eagerly sought by hunters. I haven't hunted in years, but instinctively my arms swung up, as if bringing a shotgun to the ready. But as I watched the birds fly off, I found myself hoping no hunters climb that hill this year.

I could hear the hawk screaming long before I could see it. Red-tailed hawks love to soar above that hill, because sunshine reflecting heat off the rocky ledges creates thermal updrafts that enable the hawks, while floating on motionless wings, to circle higher and higher. They sail for hours up there when the conditions are right, so free and majestic that I, shackled as I am to the earth, am repeatedly left with equal feelings of admiration and

115

envy.

Even after I finally broke into the clearing among the ledges at the summit, it took several moments before I could locate the hawk. I had to shade my eyes against the sunshine and stare hard, but eventually I could make out a tiny speck in the sky, gliding in graceful, sweeping circles.

Even from such lofty heights, however, the hawk's cries came through loud and clear. But it was a different cry than I heard through the summer. Somehow, this one seemed less anxious, less urgent, and more exuberant, more joyful. It was as if the hawk was overwhelmed by the refreshing winds and was shouting its ecstasy.

And just as the hawk is a bird of autumn, so Rusty is a dog of autumn. Perhaps it's the hunting instincts inherited from a thousand ancestors, or maybe it's just that, with his long hair, cooler weather is so much more comfortable. Whatever the reason, he finds a new zest for life and action when fall comes.

He joined me atop the rocky ledge, after wandering all over the hilltop, and arrived out of breath. He stood there, panting, looking straight at me, and he, too, had a new expression; not one of weariness but one of deep satisfaction. If he could talk, he would have said, "Now, this is the life, isn't it, Boss?"

We lingered up there a long time. The hawk soared out of sight. The sun began slipping behind the next hill. The wind diminished to a playful breeze. Reluctantly, we headed home. Back to the overgrown lawn and tomatoes and mosquitoes. Back to the things of summer.

But we knew the corner had been turned. We knew summer was really gone. We had found autumn, up there on the hill. We had seen it and heard it and felt it. The dog, the hawk and I.

Apple aroma

It's not quite right yet, but it's getting there. Another week or two at the most, and the odor will be perfect.

Autumn in my part of the country means apple time, and the rural roads are already being clogged on weekends with crowds eager to get into the orchards. Most people pick their own apples to save a little money, or give the kids a brief look at "country life" or relive a bit of their own childhood or maybe just for an afternoon out in the sunshine and invigorating breezes.

Those are all valid reasons, but there is something else that draws me each September and October. It's the aroma. The apples are ready now; the aroma takes a little longer.

Describing that aroma is difficult. At first, it's a subtle, almost indiscernible backdrop to the laden trees, now drooping under the burden of red and gold apples. You see the apples and maybe you'll notice the scarlet leaves of Virginia creeper on the stone wall or the asters in the fencerow. You might hear the crows calling from the hillside or the bees buzzing around the fallen fruit, but the "apple smell" is just a hint, like soft background music.

Then, as the nights cool and the fruit mellows, the aroma builds and builds, until it finally fills the breezes with a cider-like fragrance that can be heady stuff indeed. Usually, it takes a hard frost to bring out the best aroma, but a series of chilly nights can produce a pretty good "harvest" too. It's getting there.

When that aroma is just right, you'll know it, and that aroma will remain in memory long after you leave the orchard. Apples picked at that time will retain the odor, too, and so will cider. Later, whenever either is enjoyed, images of bronzed orchards and blue skies and frosty mornings will return as well.

Pick-your-own programs are in effect at many orchards now, and the idea is great for city people who otherwise might never get to show their kids that apples don't grow in supermarkets. It helps orchard owners, too, who often have trouble finding enough pickers, but the obvious waste and potential damage to

117

trees must make them reluctant to open orchards to the public.

Apples are too valuable to be tromped on and left lying, smashed, in the grass, and the trees are far too important to suffer the broken branches and scarred trunks so many are left with when the picking season ends.

Such problems now have forced some orchard owners to ban very young children from taking part in the picking, and nearly all ask that trees not be climbed. Unfortunately, both precautions are necessary. If you're planning to pick your own apples this year, please treat both the trees and the fruit with the proper respect.

Right now, early in the season, apples are still picked easily from the ground and there is no need to climb the trees. As the season wears on, it will take a little more time and a little more effort to get your half-bushel or bushel filled. But by then you'll get more than just fruit and exercise for your trip to the country — you'll have that apple aroma to remember. That could be worth almost as much as the apples.

A satisfying summation

Now it's October, the time for the silent walker of the night to begin roaming again. It hasn't been around since early last spring, but the time is short now.

Frost is about to arrive once more, putting an end to the growing season and signaling the start of the storing season. One frost doesn't plunge the countryside into winter, but it does mean that there will be no more time to grow vegetables, no more time to enjoy the dazzling zinnias. It means the things of summer should be put aside and some thought given to the things of winter.

Countrymen close to their soil watch for the warnings of first frost, and not necessarily in newspapers or television. They notice the foggy mist in the hollows at dusk. They hear the murmur in the coloring leaves. They feel the newness of the October air. They sense the restlessness of the animals and birds.

Men with gardens then get out wheelbarrows and baskets and begin the final harvest. The last of the tomatoes are collected. The remaining carrots and cabbages and beets and onions are added to the mound. Fat squashes and pumpkins are saved for the second load. Then potatoes are dug.

The work is done without the regret usually associated with the end of summer and approach of frost. The final harvest is a satisfying summation to an annual cycle. It even feels good to jerk out the tomato vines, to cut the corn stalks that have been standing bare for weeks, to add the withering pumpkin vines to the compost pile.

Then the frost comes. It picks a windless night when the stars lean close, and quietly steals across the land. It travels the valleys first, and lingers in the low meadows. It wanders aimlessly, stepping over woodlots and resting on flowerbeds, nibbling grasses in the open yard and ignoring rose vines hiding in the house's shadow.

By dawn, the frost's path can be read by the glistening on the weed stalks and the blackening of the morning glory vines, hanging limp and languid. Early sunshine sets the grass shimmering, and turns the spider web into sparkling crystal. Tree leaves are curled and crickets are stilled and the light breeze coming through the woods creates more of a rustle than yesterday.

In a matter of hours, however, or even minutes, the sunshine erases the white from the grass. The spider web is just a spider web again. But there is no reprieve for the morning glories. And once that first frost walks the night, there is no turning back for autumn. The pattern is set. The year has started on the long slope toward winter.

The fox, wild and free

It's a sound to listen for in the night. It comes from far off, perhaps across the valley, from some hillside pasture, or maybe from the pile of boulders up in the woods.

The fox is back.

There is seldom a shortage of foxes in the countryside, but for the most part, they're secretive, unobtrusive. You'll hardly ever see one. In fact, you might never know they were around if they didn't leave tracks in the snow. Of if they didn't bark in these crisp autumn nights.

Red foxes don't really howl — not in the way coyotes howl — but they can't resist a little barking each fall. It's a rather high-pitched yip, a timeless sound of the wild and free. They seem to bark out of sheer ecstasy. Why shouldn't they be happy? They have survived decades of hunting and trapping. They have survived encroaching civilization and subdivisions and roaming dogs.

From the time I happened to see "my fox" that morning several years ago, prancing across an abandoned pasture, she was something special. She seemed to float, sometimes trotting with effortless grace, sometimes practically dancing on her hind legs as she tried to see over the tall weeds and grasses. Frequently, she'd stop, the pounce, probably after a mouse. Then she'd be off again, ears erect, white-tipped tail in the wind. She was beautiful.

But there was no certainty she would be back this fall. She had dug her den beneath a huge boulder in a clearing high on the hill last spring, and apparently had her pups there. But the den was vacated early — too early for the pups to be grown, it seemed — and I wondered whether the increased human traffic in the area was becoming too much for her.

With the help of Rusty and his inquisitive nose, numerous other fox haunts were checked during the summer. We scrambled over boulders. We wandered around meadows. Rusty was called to every burrow and each likely den beneath the rocks. His immediate disinterest told the story. All were empty. The fox was

123

gone.

Foxes are wanderers. Even when the youngsters are in the den, the parents may roam many miles in their night foraging. And when the pups disperse at the end of summer, some will relocate as far as a hundred miles away. The males, in particular, like to see new country.

So there's no way of knowing whether the fox yipping up on the hill the other night was the same one that spent last winter there. But it's pleasant thinking that an old friend has returned.

Last winter, her tracks showed that she zig-zagged down across the pasture nearly every night. She'd scratch out a mouse, then she'd follow a rabbit trail. She'd visit the stream, and when there was ice, she'd poke around the muskrat lodge in the marsh. Occasionally, she would cross over to some backyards, sometimes going right up to bird feeders, especially if suet had been put out there.

Whether this fox does the same, or even if it stays, remains to be seen. For now, though, it's enough that she, or he, is up there. It's good to hear the barking again.

Gathering memories

This year our race with the squirrels for the walnuts and hickory nuts seems to be a draw. But I certainly can't complain about that; it's the best we've done for some time.

There are numerous hickories up on the hillside and a small grove of walnuts halfway down the slope, but in most years our take is pretty small. The squirrels get there first.

This year, though, we kept a sharper eye on the nuts and started our collecting almost as soon as the squirrels did. They let us know in rather sharp language that they didn't appreciate our invasion, but there was enough to go around. It's been a very good years in those trees.

Gathering nuts in mid-October is something of a ritual for us, akin to taking a walk in the first snow storm, and listening for the first spring peepers, and searching for the first marsh marigolds, and picking the first wild raspberries. October just wouldn't be the same without the nuts.

It's a family project. We go out some crisp, bright afternoon, usually a Sunday, when the breeze is whispering through the treetops and already carrying the tantalizing aroma of leaf smoke. We take a five-gallon bucket, hike up past the marsh, now ablaze with its glowing maples and sumac, and climb the slope. The kids do most of the work, scurrying around in the fallen leaves just like the squirrels. And just like we did a few years ago.

Then, if it's hickory nuts we're collecting, we sit on logs and hull them. We listen to the squirrels screaming at us from the branches and I start remembering how I used to fill a five-gallon bucket for my father, and Bettie tells how she and her parents used burlap sacks. It seems those who collect nuts also collect memories.

With walnuts, the hulls are too tough for immediate shucking, so we take them home and spread them out in the basement to dry. Later, we'll use the vise or a hammer and break them open. They're good, too, particularly in cookies and cakes, but not quite up to the hickories.

There are a few hazelnut bushes up on the hillside, and a couple of butternut trees, and even a chestnut or two, but we gather only enough of those nuts for a taste. They don't seem as important as the hickories.

So this year we got busy right along with the squirrels. When they get first crack, they usually leave only the wormy ones for us. This year we filled that bucket a couple of times, left plenty for the squirrels, and collected some memories of October woodlands. It's been a very good year.

Old Lewie and winter's signs

Old Lewie never turned to television or newspapers when he wanted a weather forecast. He just checked the spiders, or woolly bears, or hornets, or hickory nuts, or muskrats, or fog, or smoke, or thunder.

In early October, men like Old Lewie—countrymen close to their land—would carefully observe the natural happenings around them. It was a sure way to predict what kind of winter lay ahead, they insisted.

Old Lewie no longer lives across the meadow, as he did for so many years, but each autumn we still seek out his barometers for our own extended forecast. They're even better than the *Old Farmer's Almanac*. Old Lewie could tell exactly how many snowstorms would be coming. Of course, he wasn't always right.

The last year he lived near us, for example, he said the winter would be free of "real" storms because August had been free of heavy fogs up our way. That was the year of the Great Blizzard, and even Lewie had to admit that was a "real" storm. He tried to get around our needling by saying there must have been a heavy fog along the coastline that he didn't take into account.

That's one of nature's signs. The number of heavy fogs in August reveals how many storms will hit in winter. That's what Old Lewie said.

Another is that well-known symbol of folklore, the woolly bear caterpillar. The little caterpillars that scrinch along on sunny fall days are black on each end with a band of red-brown around the middle. The width of the band supposedly tells whether the winter is to be severe or mild, but most countrymen have trouble agreeing—or remembering—which is which. Anyway, a wide band means something, and the winter will be extremely bad if you see the woolly bear out crawling before the first frost.

Lots of spiders wandering around in fall means a tough winter ahead, and we have had lots of spiders. We also have many hornets all over the yard, but that in itself is not as dire a sign as their nests. Thicker walls than usual are the thing to look for here, but so far the hornets have been too busy for us to check the nest walls that closely. Come to think of it, though, the nests do seem closer to the ground this year, and that's another sign of trouble ahead. That's what Old Lewie said.

Hickory nuts don't sting, so we can check out their predictions very easily. They, too, are said to have thicker shells if cruel weather lies ahead. Maybe we can all relax, because the hickory shells seem no thicker than usual. We think.

Of course, the muskrats are saying we better batten down for a real toughie. Down in the marshes, they are building their lodges high and solid, a sure sign of impending storms.

You don't even have to visit the marshes, though. Lots of rolling thunder in fall means a severe winter is coming, and you can tell exactly when snow is coming just by watching the smoke from your chimney. According to Old Lewie, if smoke flows down and settles on the ground, it will snow in 26 days. That's what Old Lewie said.

There are more signs, too. Thicker hair on cows and horses. Heavier husk on ears of corn. More but smaller acorns. Crows gathering earlier than usual. Carrots growing deeper. Big crops of dogwood berries. A later first frost than normal. Tough skins on sweet potatoes. Crickets in cellars already by this time.

If you notice any or all of the above, you'd better buy new snow tires and take out a loan for more heating oil, because, baby, it's gonna be cold outside. At least, that's what Old Lewie said.

It's a grape year

It doesn't seem to happen often — maybe once every five or six years — but this appears to be the time. It's a grape year.

Wild grapes, that is.

Right now, those big, purple bunches they call fox grapes are at their peak. Find the right spot, and you can fill buckets and buckets with the sweet, thick-skinned fruit in just minutes. They're perfect for making jelly.

Fox grapes are the ancestors of the Concord, Catawba and several other varieties of domestic grapes — and cannot match those in the arbor for most uses — but they're still worth picking, especially if you like grape jelly.

Of course, there are other reasons, too.

One is the aroma. It's the smell of autumn, just as surely as the fragrance of green hickory nuts, or apples after the first hard frost, or the whiff of distant wood smoke. The smells of the season. None is as heady as lilacs in May or new-mown hay in July, but they are as tantalizing in a more subtle way. And just as irresistible to those who know them.

Another reason to pick wild grapes is, simply, that they are wild, and gathering them enables you to become part of the wild scene in a small way. The vines sprawl all over bushes and stone walls and even trees, and sometimes the competition for the grapes is lively indeed. Chances are, years after you've forgotten how many pounds of fruit you picked, you'll remember the raccoon with purple-stained paws, or the possum you surprised in the vine, or maybe even the fox so engrossed in gobbling up grapes that it didn't hear you approach. It happens.

Fox grapes are easy to find — they virtually blanket all vegetation along many rural roads — but more often than not they are mostly leaves and few grapes. Many years, there are no grapes at all.

But this fall the fruit is thick in favored places and the biggest problem is trying to reach the grapes on vines that have crawled high in the trees. Don't worry if you cannot pick them;

they won't go to waste. Raccoons climb very well, you know.

We now have our own arbor, and those grapes were picked a couple of weeks ago, but still we have to go out and search for the wild bunches. It's become something of a tradition, maybe even a ritual, a way of welcoming autumn, just as we sometimes neglect our own strawberries in early spring to look for tiny wild strawberries back in some abandoned pasture.

Gathering wild fruit has a special significance; it provides a needed link with a country heritage. For centuries, rural folk have reaped the harvest of the woods and roadsides and marshes. Because the northeast is not well suited for grapes, bountiful Septembers were few, but that only made the good years — like this one — all the more special.

At the same time, the grapes keep you in tune with the seasonal changes. The "winey" aroma. The chilled breezes. The scolding squirrels. The nervous birds. All fairly shout of autumn. Such elements should not be missed.

And that jelly comes in handy, too.

First frost

You'd know it even if you couldn't feel the cold. You step outside and immediately it hits you — the season has changed. First frost.

It arrived as it always does; not with a roar but with silent stealth. It picks a calm, clear night and slips down the hillsides as softly as the darkness itself. But by dawn, its presence is seen, heard, smelled and felt.

Those accustomed to walking early might first notice the sounds — there aren't any. On the morning after the first hard frost, there is silence across the countryside. For the first time in months, there are no insects droning, no frogs bellowing, no whip-poorwills or other birds calling.

It may take you a second to realize just what the difference is, but you'll know something has changed.

In a few hours, when the sunshine has returned a bit of warmth, the chilled creatures will stir once again and sounds will resume — bees buzzing and crickets creaking and a hundred birds chirping and twittering and squabbling and cawing. But in the thin dawn light, all is quiet.

Obviously, the biggest difference is that delicate, white coating all over the yard. Each blade of grass, each leaf, each exposed pine needle is sheathed in fragile crystalline frost. It melts the moment the sunshine hits, but until then it is beauty of a quality man has never been able to duplicate.

On these first-frost mornings, I like to stroll out through the garden and to the meadow beyond. That's where the most exquisite sights are found, out in the open areas where the frost has had a chance to rest comfortably.

Usually, there are leaves lying in the garden, and not many scenes are more spectacular than a maple leaf, still painted scarlet or orange, fringed in frosty filigree. And the blackberry leaves, now a deep crimson, shimmer with their transparent silver coating. It's enough to make the limp, blackened vines of the nearby tomatoes easier to take.

Out in the meadow, I always notice the goldenrods first. Overnight, they have been transformed from proud, golden-maned warriors into aging soldiers, bowed and gray. Some of the asters, too, seem a bit frayed around the edges although many survive the first frost if they have any shelter at all.

Walk in the crisp, nippy dawn and the air even smells different. Somehow, it's cleaner, sharper. It's too soon for the frost to have an effect on the apples and grapes — that aroma will come in a couple of days — but there is something different out there. Maybe it's just the settling of other smells. Maybe it's the anticipation of new fragrances. Maybe it's just the frost itself. Maybe it's just autumn.

And if you feel close to the land, you'll recognize the new feeling that first frost introduces. It's a little sad, a little melancholy, but it's also exciting and invigorating. Each season change is. Another milestone has been passed. Growing season — unless you covered your tomatoes and flowers — has ended. Now it's time to start thinking of gathering and storing, putting away the things of summer.

First frost tells you those geese that went over last week weren't jumping the gun after all; that those chipmunks and squirrels under the oaks knew what they were doing; that the flickers flocking in the woods have a reason for looking so eager to be off.

It always seems those things are too early; it can't be time yet to be so deep into autumn. But now the line of demarcation has been crossed. It will be warm again — there's always an Indian summer — but it's finally sinking in that there can be no turning back now. Not after first frost.

The foreverness of October

There are days in autumn when time seems to stand still. In this foreverness of October, winter seems far away. In fact, so do the other seasons. Walk the woodlands and fields now, and it's as if they always will be autumn. Always beautiful. Always invigorating. Always satisfying.

In a month or less, another shift in the seasons will silence the insects and frogs. It will wither the last wildflowers. It will send migrant birds off on long journeys. It will fade the golden leaves, and drop them to the ground.

I know all that, and yet it becomes hard to believe as I wander the countryside. All around is maturity, fulfillment, contentment. The brilliant sunshine and cloudless skies, the stirring breezes and poignant aromas can cast a spell — they say this is the way the world should be. Knowing that fall won't last much longer should make it fly by, but for some reason it doesn't work that way.

Stroll through a meadow or pasture. Crickets scurry across the paths. Grasshoppers leap from dry weeds. Dragonflies hover and dart, like miniature helicopters. Honey bees are so eagerly collecting pollen from the asters that each bee appears to be wearing bright yellow saddlebags.

Do these insects know their time is growing short? Of course not. They are living now. Nothing else matters.

Sparrows in the brush, and the first juncos down from the north, are quietly searching out seeds, but towhees greet me with their cheery whistles. Towhees will be pulling out any day, but they show no signs of leaving just yet. What's the hurry?

Crows flap by overhead, screaming all the while. Blue jays at the edge of the woods try to keep pace, jeering loudly at me, at the crows and at each other. Chickadees, too, are noisy. They seem to love this time of year. But then, they seem to enjoy every season, don't they?

The trail going into the woods is littered now with acorns and leaves, and a chipmunk is there, sounding as huge as a dog as it bustles around. He bounds onto a rock, and glares at me. One cheek pouch is so filled it nearly squeezes his eye shut. The other cheek also is bulging; the chipmunk seems to have three heads. He takes a couple of quick, jerky steps, stamps his feet, and somehow — even with his mouth full — manages to scream an expletive or two before diving beneath a rock.

I find myself stopping often and just looking and listening. The more spectacular colors of autumn have given way to a softer golden glow. Sassafras. Hickory. Birch. Some of the earlier beeches. There's as much of a glow coming from the forest floor, too, with ferns and other ground-hugging plants showing off their own fall costumes. They aren't noticed when maples are afire with orange and red, but now there is time for the lesser lights.

Time. It seems to linger like haze on the hillsides, like mist above the hollows. It drifts as slowly and softly as butterflies, and is as reluctant to let go of the season.

On these magical days, it seems October really is forever, and that's not a bad idea at all.

Between harvest and hoarfrost

There are two times of year that should be spent on a farm. One is spring — April and May — when there is new life bursting around you every day. The other is now — October — when that season of growth has reached maturity.

October is the year at harvest. Pumpkins, plump and hardy, rest in their patches, looking relieved to be finished with their frantic summer of growth. Apples similarly have reached maturity, and await picking. So have the grapes. They've never looked better.

The long rows of corn stand silent, bronzed and sere, their golden grain secure. Now that I don't have to husk the corn by hand any more, I miss the old-fashioned shocks in the fields. Those teepee-shaped shocks lent substance to the term "Indian summer." In the hazy evenings of late October, it was easy for children to imagine the fields were Indian villages, particularly with leaves blowing about and distant wood smoke in the air.

There is more burnished bronze than vibrant green around the farm in October, more fragrance than fertilizer, more serenity than sweat, and alas, usually more pride than profit.

A farm in October is horses reaching over the fence toward the fallen apples and cattle munching contentedly on browning grass, and when allowed, on corn fodder. It is chickens scratching around in the new wood ashes dumped out back and dogs straining at leashes, eager to roam the hillsides.

October is quail in the fencerows and foxes nosing around the chicken coop. It is grouse hiding in the cedars and migrant warblers passing through the woodlots. It is crows preaching from the treetops and owls calling in the darkness and geese silhouetted against a golden moon.

October is asters decorating the pasture and sumac branches ablaze and the annual festival of colors in the trees that by the month's end will see fallen leaves ankle-deep on the woods path. It is squirrels and chipmunks dashing about gathering acorns, and mice searching for winter quarters. It is woodchucks

135

fattening themselves for hibernation. It is deer dallying in the orchard at dawn, feasting on windfall apples.

And there are the aromas. The orchard and the arbor and the woods offer their own toasts to the season. October, here's to you. Here's to the heady fragrance of the frost-kissed apples, the winey smell of ripened grapes, the wild-as-the-wind smell of hickory nuts. And the nostalgic whiff of that first wood smoke — which is now common again since the resurrection of wood stoves — is a delight, although you certainly don't have to live in the country to know that aroma these days.

But you won't know the quail and the cows and the asters in the city. You won't hear the owls or the foxes or the high-flying geese. And you won't really know October unless you are out there where the sunshine and the frost and the season itself control life and lives. Now, between harvest and hoarfrost, anyone who has spent time on a farm remembers. And, in October, most of us long to return.

Special trees

At this time of year, everybody should have his own special tree. Or maybe a grove of them. Or perhaps a whole hillside.

It's not really necessary to own that tree legally, as in formal deeds and town hall records and all that. You can "own" a tree simply by paying attention to it as it progresses through October's season of change, and appreciating what transpires.

For example, there is a swamp maple near a marsh that I pass every day. That is "my" tree almost as surely as the little maples in my own yard. I look for it each time I go by, and never fail to note how much it resembles a huge mound of molten gold. Now, with some of the leaves already falling, it looks as though so much gold was poured over it the excess is dripping onto the ground.

There is another maple, this one a sugar maple, in a neighbor's yard that I have claimed as my own. The colors are different each year, and change practically day by day, so it is truly a tree of wonder. There are brilliant displays of crimson and scarlet one year, then a dazzling array of gold and orange the next, and sometimes a mixture of them all. When the sunshine hits that tree just right, it looms like a beacon on the slope. My neighbor rakes up those leaves in November, but in October it's my tree, too.

I have other special trees as well. Down near the river is a thick grove of dogwoods, trees that lure me in spring when they are gowned in showy white blossoms. I have to go back each October for another look, because now the dogwoods are blood-red, and there is the bonus of the shiny red berry clusters. Squirrels like dogwoods, too, but they evidently are more interested in collecting the berries for food than appreciating the crimson leaves.

On the same hillside, up near the rocky ledges, are sassafras saplings, and they are mine, too, in autumn. Right now, sassafras leaves are blazing, each bough aflame with gold, adding as warm a glow to the rocks as these early-evening fires add warming glows on the hearth.

But if I had to choose one tree to own each autumn, it would be an old black tupelo, or black gum, that I discovered years ago on a nearby hilltop. It grows beside a little pond, hidden far beyond the sight of passing motorists. Getting to it requires a half-hour climb up a steep, slippery path, but I have to make that climb each October. I just have to.

The tree is not particularly tall, or well-shaped. In fact, a big limb has broken off one side and it is now leaning precariously out over the tiny pool. But it is a masterpiece nevertheless.

The word "red" is woefully inadequate in describing its leaves. Each leaf, it seems, struggles mightily to reach a richer, more vivid, shade of scarlet than the next. The tree lights up the whole hillside, putting to shame the younger maples and oaks and ashes that crowd around it like adoring children.

When I go up there, I pause on a rock on the opposite side of the pond and just look. Sometimes I catch it when the leaves are starting to drop, one by one, into the water below, and I think of rubies falling from some gigantic treasure chest. Some trees can do things like that to the imagination.

The hill and woods are not mine, nor are the pond and the boulders. But that tree is mine. Every October.

And when it finally falls, no one will feel its loss more. But it will still be mine, at least in memory.

No time to dally

Back and forth he swims. There is no time for resting. Maybe the other creatures of the marsh can take it easy, but not the old muskrat.

It's mid-October now, and the muskrat doesn't need a calendar to tell him what that means. He doesn't need to hear the gabbling geese crossing overhead in the night either, or to see the dazzling color displays in the maples.

He can tell by the chill in the water, the crispness in the air. And by a thing called instinct. They tell him it's time to get ready for winter, constructing a beaver-style lodge far out in the marsh.

A flock of wood ducks comes in and noisily explores the shallow water's bottom. A few months ago, the muskrat would have been right there with the ducks, hoping to snatch an unsuspecting youngster. But now it's October, not June. He doesn't even look.

A wandering kingfisher rattles excitedly from a high branch. The muskrat pays no attention. Not even the presence of a gaunt blue heron, which stands four feet tall, can get the muskrat to slow down. He has a job to do, and it's time to do it.

Cattails are cut down and pulled through the water to the lodge. So are arrowhead stalks and small limbs gnawed off driftwood. Slowly the mound out in the marsh grows. It looks like a haphazard trash pile, but the muskrat knows what he's doing.

Each time he jams a cattail stalk into the mound, he disappears under water for a few moments, going inside the pile to check on the progress. There's a big room in the middle of that pile and he's going to spend the entire winter there, so he wants it just right.

For the finishing touches, which sometimes come several days after the project is started, the muskrat plasters the exterior of the mound with mud. It's his insulation, and when it freezes solid later, it will be an impregnable wall that will discourage marauding foxes and dogs and raccoons.

The muskrat's chamber will be above the water line, but the

entrances and exits all will be under water, and he won't have to show his face all winter if so desired, except to poke a nose through the air holes every so often. Food will be abundant down there, in the form of water weed stems and roots, and he'll be safe and snug, far better off than most wild mammals.

But the lodge won't get built by itself, so while the ducks and kingfisher jabber, he works. He knows what time it is.

Winter wheat

W heat—that grain that feeds most of America and half of the rest of the world—is keeping one family in touch with its heritage. My family.

Our "field" is just a 20-foot-by-10-foot strip along the edge of the garden, but the size doesn't really matter. We've sown our winter wheat; our link with the open farmlands of the midwest remains intact.

Actually, we haven't farmed all that much since moving to Rhode Island, and the subtle but very real values—aesthetic as well as economic—of something like wheat were gradually being forgotten. Our views of farming were narrowing into summer trips back to Ohio, and summer's time-of-plenty on the farm is rather deceiving.

Our kids were beginning to think of farming as only harvesting; reaping the bounty. They've seen hay being baled and soybeans being combined and tomatoes being picked. They know the rows of corn stalks stretch for miles out there, and the endless expanses of wheat ripple in the breezes like a golden sea. But they never see the fall plowing—or the winter waiting.

And without knowing those other seasons, they will never know farming.

This year, though, they may get a better idea of what it's all about.

Our last trip there, in July, happened to be right in the middle of the wheat combining season, and despite the drought that hurt other crops, the grain harvest was staggering. Tractors and combines clattered almost around the clock, hurrying to gather the precious gold before the demon all wheat farmers fear—a hailstorm—could strike.

On the spur of the moment, we visited an old buddy of mine, Jerry Hilvers, who calls himself Ohio's best farmer. In fact, I think he called himself that when we first met back in the first grade. He's a burly bear of a man, with arms like oak limbs and a handshake that could crush rocks.

And he's never really forgiven me for deserting "God's country" for the east. So every time we visit he does a selling job on the kids, rattling off the virtues of farm life, and expressing shock over just how little eastern kids know about growing things.

This time, he gave my sons a bag of wheat, and when they asked what to do with it, he was properly baffled. Plant it, of course, he told them. Grow your own wheat next summer. Show Rhode Island what good Ohio grain looks like.

He even said he'd write them when it was time to plow the field and plant the stuff.

Jerry doesn't forget. His letter came last week, with planting instructions, and the boys quickly prepared and sowed their pocket-sized field.

My wife and I, both products of farms, watched with mild amusement, but the more we thought about having our own wheat patch again, the more we liked the idea.

Winter wheat has that special quality that farmers—or anybody close to the land and its workings—need. Planted in early October, it is up and green before the freeze-up and snows come.

All winter, when the other fields are drab and barren, and summer's bounty seems so far away, the wheat field stays green and vibrant. It is a touch of life, of promise, amid all the bleakness that can become bleaker each day to the waiting farmer.

He will tell you winter wheat is important because it nourishes the soil, and prevents wind and rain erosion, and eventually may produce another harvest like last July's, but he knows it is more than that.

He knows that having that one field of green out there is his assurance that another spring will be coming, another season of sunshine and growing and reaping. It's his promise that next year will be the best ever. It's his proof that hope—for the most independent, most individualistic of all workers—does, indeed, spring eternal.

It's a lesson I hope our little field imparts to two eastern boys whose roots go back to Ohio. The lesson of the wheat.

Gabble of the geese

It doesn't seem to happen that often any more; maybe that's why it is so special. Now, every flock of geese noticed crossing high overhead is an event, a lucky occurrence to talk about and relish and remember.

The gabbling of the migrating geese has long been considered the song of autumn itself, a bittersweet voice of restlessness and freedom and, yes, a warning of what lies ahead. When the big geese desert us for the south, winter and ice and cold are on the horizon.

But how many people these days hear the geese? They still make the flights each fall; they still keep up their constant honking as they go. But now the noise — that delightful, yet haunting, clamor of the skies — is usually drowned out by the din down here below. Or simply ignored.

Already, some of the geese are on the move; it's getting cold up north where they live. They may not be in full migration just yet, but they're feeling that restlessness and are gradually moving down the coast, lingering for days or weeks at times on comfortable ponds.

When they are given the signal to head south — and they are better weather predictors than most human meteorologists — they'll launch into the sky, make their V formation, with one leg of the V invariably longer than the other, and depart. If the weather is clear at the time, they may fly so high they are mere specks to the earthbound observers, and therefore it would be easy to understand how a great many pass unnoticed.

But the geese's gabbling has always been what attracted attention. The man working in his woodlot and the woman in her garden would hear the clamor when it was still far in the distance, a faint rumble that seemed to echo from all parts of the sky at once.

Immediately, they would look up, searching hard for those geese. The axe would fall silent and the shovel would be momentarily forgotten. All eyes swept the heavens until the flock was

145

found. Not until the last goose vanished on the southern horizon would work be resumed.

And when such a flock has passed, it's difficult to dismiss them from the mind. The geese are both exhilarating and a bit sad. Most of us who see them are stirred by their vibrant wildness; we envy their footloose mobility. If only we were as free as the wild geese. But the fading echo of their gabble also is the echo of another summer gone, another flock of birds driven from us.

Now, the geese are most easily noticed at night and at dawn, when the daytime roar of modern living is as its lowest volume. Then, if you're lucky, you might hear that unmistakable voice of autumn. Take the time to look up. In the first rays of day the geese are painted gold. At night, they can be silhouetted against a bright yellow moon. That's a sight for artists and poets, and is not often actually seen, but when it is, it's never to be forgotten.

The ancient oaks

Will this be the last year for the old oaks? Their last few acorns? Their final autumn of holding on to their leathery leaves until well after the snow flies?

The two old monarchs stand a few miles apart in the northern part of the state. Even though both are immense, they are hidden from view, surrounded by younger, more vigorous trees. They have been there for many decades, silently keeping watch over the nearby hillsides and ponds and fields.

Those oaks may have been there when redmen yielded to the inevitable and relinquished their homeland to a new race. They were there when the hillside—now a dense forest—served several struggling farms. They were there when some of those farm boys marched off to war, first a war for independence and then a war for national unity.

They were there when the farmers at last abandoned the land, and they were there when the last of the buildings fell in, when new trees sprouted in the pastures, when the last traces of human inhabitation—save for the timeless stone walls—were obliterated.

Both massive oaks stand beside stone walls, which probably is why they were saved when the hill was cleared all those years ago. Farmers liked to leave an occasional big tree standing if it was out of the way—often next to a wall—to provide shade for their livestock. Such trees were a blessing for the farmers themselves, too, during hot days of hand labor in the fields. Nearly every farm had several.

Through the decades, the two giant trees seemed immortal. They would last as long as the stone walls stood, it seemed. But now, the trees are showing their age.

One has only a few small branches at the top still alive. Lower limbs, which stretch out far in each direction, have been dead for so long there are pines, some already 40 feet tall, growing between the long-reaching but bare arms. The trunk is scarred from some long-forgotten fire. A hollow branch just above the crotch

147

has been home for generations of raccoons.

This tree's days, apparently, are numbered. Decay in the lower limbs must reach the upper branches soon. Perhaps a heavy snowfall or wind storm, or maybe lightning, will topple the entire tree first.

That might be a blessing. I would not want to see the grand old tree rot away, limb by limb, crippled anew by each succeeding season. It deserves better.

The other tree is doing better, although it, too, has several dead branches. It's one of the largest trees in this state, more than 22 feet around its trunk. Some of the lower limbs are nearly four feet thick. Horizontal branches reach out about 40 feet, and they have held the encroaching forest at bay all these years. Only a few bushes and saplings grow within its circle; its thick canopy has kept all other trees from gaining a start.

"Majestic" is the word that comes to mind every time I see it. So big. So old. So proud.

How many hundreds of thousands of leaves has it produced? How many acorns? How many cows and horses stood in its shade? How many people paused there to rest? To gaze across the pond below? How many kids climbed its branches, then grew old and departed, while the tree remained?

How many other trees sprouted, withered and died in futile competition with it? How many oaks farther down the hill were the result of its acorns rolling away from the parent tree? How many squirrels and chipmunks and birds were fed by those acorns?

And now, I wonder, how much longer will the tree survive?

This year, I paused beneath the tree one more time, and picked up two of its acorns. If this is, indeed, its last year, I want to keep one of the acorns. The other one, I will plant.

Seeking autumn answers

Now, when the evenings grow long and the fireside hearth beckons, there is <u>time to ponder</u>—but not too deeply—some of the basic questions of autumn.

Why, for instance, are the oaks wearing such vivid red foliage this year, far brighter than their usual red-brown? And why have the dogwood leaves hung on so long? They should have been down weeks ago.

How can mockingbirds and cardinals, which moved up here from the south relatively recently, fare so well during our winters, while orioles and tanagers, which have been nesting here for centuries, still must desert us each fall?

Do woodchucks, still stuffing themselves for hibernation, ever become too fat to move when Indian Summer drags autumn out extra long? Do chipmunks ever run out of storage area?

Why is the crop of hickory nuts somewhat better this year? And why do the largest oak trees seem to have the smallest acorns?

What is the reason for the little wintergreen plants producing their berries now? Is it simply to feed the grouse and other wildlife? And why don't more animals and birds eat those orange berries on the plant called bittersweet? Most hang on the vines all winter.

Why do we still change the clocks twice a year? And if we must make changes, wouldn't it make more sense to reverse the process, adding the extra hour to the evenings in winter, when we could really use it, rather than summer, when we have plenty of daylight?

Wouldn't it be a good idea to allow each family, or at least each neighborhood, <u>one leaf-fire a year</u>, just for the fragrance and nostalgia? Would that really be more dangerous and polluting than all the wood-stove fires?

What system do the chickadees have in spreading the word about new feeding stations being opened in the area? Do the acrobatic nuthatches, which are upside down most of the time as they prowl tree limbs, ever fall on their heads?

Are crows really blacker now, and blue jays bluer, or is it just a matter of their surroundings becoming duller as the leaves fade and fall? How about the pines; are their new needles greener than the summer needles? It seems that way. And do new needles push out the old? The pines are standing ankle-deep in browning needles, but the transition goes so smoothly we never notice it.

Did all the turtles and frogs and salamanders find safe places to sleep away the winter? How about all the spiders and beetles and bumblebees? If the grubs and larvae ever learned to hide better, would the woodpeckers and nuthatches starve?

Why do the stars seem so much clearer and so much closer now than in summer? Why does the constellation Orion, now brilliant before dawn, always bring such a comforting feeling? It's like recognizing an old friend.

Is there a wilder, and yet more poignant, sound now than an owl calling in the darkness? Why do the red foxes up on the hill seem to have such hoarse voices? They just started yipping; they shouldn't have sore throats already.

Why must November weather change so quickly? Why do the winds have such a cutting edge at this time of year? And why is it always windiest on soccer and football fields?

Is our own link to the past the reason for cherishing the fireplace? There are so many more efficient ways to heat; why do we insist on an open fire? It seems to warm the soul more than the body. Why?

Bittersweet season

It is a way of bringing autumn indoors, and holding on to it for awhile. All it takes is decorating the fireplace mantel with a vine of bittersweet. Both the plant and its name symbolize the season perfectly.

Late October is bittersweet indeed. Our most glorious time is passing too quickly, and November, sometimes one of our bleakest months, is already on the horizon. Indian Summer is a time to cherish; November's winds and cold rains cut through to the bone, like those of March.

It's a bittersweet season, and bittersweet berries are just right for this momentary lull. The vines often swarm all over trees—usually old, venerable monarchs—and right now, with the berries fairly glowing in their bright orange shells, they look like lights on some gray, brooding Christmas trees. Later, the shells will split open and fall—a process speeded up considerably on vines brought indoors—and reveal brilliant red berries that remain most of the winter.

Henry David Thoreau was so impressed with the berries he wrote, "I do not know of any cluster more graceful and beautiful than these droping cymes of scented or translucent, cherry-colored, elliptical berries."

Bittersweet, also called woody nightshade, has become almost too popular as an indoor decoration. In some places, so much has been pulled up that the vines are becoming hard to find. So, if you want to add this outdoorsy touch, clip only a few feet from the end of a vine, and be careful not to damage the parent vine itself.

Some wild creatures need those berries, too. Grouse, pheasants and quail often feed on them during winter's hungry days, and sometimes songbirds—waxwings, grosbeaks or wintering robins—will remain near the vines for days at a time. Squirrels, rabbits and even foxes eat the berries as well.

But don't you eat them; they're poisonous to humans.

At one time, people did search for the plant because a juicy substance inside the twig was the basis for a home remedy used to treat skin diseases. But that time is long gone. Now, the vines grow in oblivion all summer, and it is only when those berries light up, and the surrounding foliage display fades, that the plant is even noticed.

However, whether you bring a vine indoors or not, the bittersweet is worth noting. Those berries seem to brighten as the surrounding foliage withers, and as the chilling rains arrive, they serve as one of our last reminders of all of October's color. Autumn is so beautiful, but the glory leads to barrenness. It truly is a bittersweet season.

Chickadee days

These are chickadee days. When the temperature drops and the November winds blow and foreboding clouds carry a hint of snow, the chickadee comes to his time of glory. He seems to take it as a personal responsibility to keep the countryside from growing too bleak, too lifeless. He usually succeeds.

All summer he remained in the background, tending to family duties up in the hillside woods. Then, warblers and orioles and swallows and tanagers held center stage. They sang and soared and showed off their bright feathers and it was easy to forget about the little chickadee.

But now those others have deserted our part of the country for warmer weather, and the chickadee is the star of the show, and he knows it. Anybody with a bird feeder is familiar with this jaunty, black-capped beggar. Put out a handful of sunflower seeds and he'll appear, almost like magic. He'll make dozens of trips to the feeder a day, but nobody minds. He's such a friendly, entertaining little fellow he pays for his meals with each appearance.

Those of us who still cut firewood with a bow saw or axe know the chickadee well, too. He is nosy enough to investigate the sounds of men working in his woods, and ham enough to flutter about in the trees just above our heads, chirping and twittering and performing acrobatic maneuvers in the branches. He seems to like human company and will linger long, sometimes even moving with the workers as they shift from place to place. He has even become accustomed to chain saws in some areas, but the loud roar drowns out his happy song and, without top billing, he will soon move on to more appreciative audiences.

The chickadee is so gregarious for another reason—he simply can't stand still. This tiny fellow—a full-grown chickadee seldom weighs more than half an ounce—has a body temperature around 105 degrees, and his heart beats about 700 times a minute. In cold weather he needs to collect his weight in food every day. His life is frenzied activity, and frenzied activity is his life.

153

But other birds have to eat a lot, too, like nuthatches, titmice and finches. And other birds like making themselves heard. Blue jays and crows in particular. Yet, they don't have the chickadee's appeal; they don't have his personality, his spark.

He can brighten up the grayest day, whether at the window-sill feeder or in the woodlot. Add a bit of snow, and instead of retreating into silence, as most birds do, he revels in it, treating snow as something new to cheer about.

The chickadee days have begun, and thankfully, he will be around through the long months ahead. It is not pleasant thinking what winter here would be like without him. Let's hope we never find out.

Juncos

The orioles are gone for the winter. So are the thrushes, and the wrens, and the catbirds and the towhees. But all is not bleak for the birders—the juncos have arrived.

Just when the birds of summer—those flashy, boisterous, sweet-singing fair-weather birds—head south, the winter birds arrive. That means juncos, for this is their southland. And while they may not be as colorful or melodious as the orioles, they lend a cheerfulness all their own to the winter woods and meadows. Only the chickadees among our winter residents seem to retain their enthusiasm for life as much as the juncos.

For years, they were known as slate-colored juncos, which adequately described the little seed-eaters from Canada. They are dark across the head and chest, lighter underneath. Now, officially, they are dark-eyed juncos, a much more attractive, even romantic, name. But names for these birds make little difference to most people; they've always called them "snow birds."

It's an appropriate nickname, for they seem to relish snowstorms. Now and through much of the early winter, they are inconspicuous, wandering about the woods edgings and overgrown pastures. If you notice any birds back there at all, it's usually the gregarious chickadees, the raucous jays or maybe a flock of lingering yellow-rumped warblers. The juncos are there, too, but they sort of fade into the background. They're biding their time.

When snow does come, the juncos will take center stage. They'll invade backyards where feeders are set up—they aren't shy at all about accepting handouts—but usually you'll find them out in the meadows, flitting around in the snow in search of weed seeds. And looking as if they love every minute of it.

Other birds are around all winter, of course. There are the jays and woodpeckers and nuthatches. There are occasional visits by evening grosbeaks and purple finches and brown creepers. The mockingbirds and cardinals and titmice stay, and so do some crows and hawks. But nearly all of them give the impression they are not here by choice. If not bound by instinct, they'd be with the orioles and robins on the Gulf Coast. They're just tolerating our weather, not enjoying it.

Ah, but not the juncos. They act as if there is nothing better than snow in their feathers. They'll scratch around the ground when snow is not deep, looking like so many chickens in a barnyard, and ride the swaying weed stalks when the snow is deeper. They chirp and twitter and gossip among themselves as if on a picnic. Snowbirds they are indeed.

For now, though, they're content to stay in the background, just waiting. They'll come closer when the time is right—when we need them. With so many other songbirds gone, it's reassuring to know we can count on the juncos.

Beaver Moon

All the way up, as we climbed the winding trail through the woods, clouds hid the moon. But, just as we reached our goal, a rocky clearing at the summit, the clouds parted right on cue and moonlight flooded the hilltop. It was perfect.

That clearing, like any other place, takes on new dimensions at night. We went up there with hopes of hearing an owl or perhaps one of the foxes whose tracks we find every winter in the snow. Instead, we spent the visit admiring the November sky.

This was during last weekend's full moon, which in the old days was called Beaver Moon by the Indians and woodsmen. Supposedly, the reference was to both the beavers' pelts, which would be in prime condition by now for trappers, and to the animals' habits of preparing for winter. By mid-November, they had snugged their lodges and laid in enough food to last through the cold months ahead. Men were reminded to do likewise.

The moon itself lacks the golden glow and warmth of the other full moons of autumn, the Harvest Moon of September and the Hunter Moon of October. Now, the moon is white and cold, but not quite as white or as cold as those still ahead. The December moon, for instance, used to be called simply the Cold Moon, January had the Wolf Moon, and February the Hunger Moon. Winter was a difficult time, indeed; no wonder November and the Beaver Moon issued their warnings.

It was relatively mild the night we climbed the hill, and even with the cloud cover it wasn't dark enough to need a flashlight. There are few really dark nights in winter; once there is snow, the luminescence enables you to track a fox at midnight.

But now, with the trail buried in brittle, crunchy leaves, walking is too noisy. If there were any foxes or opossums or skunks or other animals about that night, they would have heard us coming a hundred yards away. So when we reached the clearing, where the moonlight was so brilliant it cast long shadows, we stopped walking, sat against a comfortable boulder and listened.

There seemed to be a couple of hoots far off in the distance, but no owls came into the clearing. Nor were there any other sounds up there. No wind. No creatures afoot. And none of the insect droning that dominated the spot during a late-night visit in September.

The moon, however, was magnificent. As the clouds parted, they took on the look of a vast snowfield, reminding us of views of houseless, trackless areas of the Midwest we had seen once from a plane. The clouds nearest the moon were bathed in an eerie, silver glow that shifted continually as the clouds hurried toward the horizon.

Tiny stars, their brightness overwhelmed by the moonlight, popped through here and there, and every few minutes we thought we saw a shooting star flash by. They were always seen out of the corners of our eyes, however, and were gone by the time we turned for a better look. Maybe they weren't there at all. Sometimes the night sky plays tricks on people.

As we sat as motionless as possible, listening and watching, we felt part of an ancient—and comforting—scene. How long has the Beaver Moon climbed across the heavens? How many times has it lighted that hill, that boulder? The stars and clouds were part of the scene, too; part of the silence and serenity. So were the owl and the fox. May it always be so.

The fickle grosbeaks

They are a status symbol—these evening grosbeaks. You can lure cardinals and chickadees and house finches to your bird feeder, but until you have evening grosbeaks, you cannot consider your feeding a total success.

Evening grosbreaks are chunky, colorful—some say gaudy—birds that travel in flocks and apparently consider themselves the gourmets of the winter bird world. They'll congregate at one feeding tray while totally ignoring another in a neighboring yard, or will show up three days in a row, then disappear for a month.

Actually, fickle is what they are.

But it's something of a coup to have them in your yard, and people who feed birds always welcome the flocks, even if they do gobble up as many sunflower seeds in an hour as the chickadees would take in several days. Let them gobble, we say. At least we have grosbeaks; the neighbors have only starlings and juncos and titmice.

That's today. Tomorrow may be a different story.

Even the name "evening" for the grosbeaks is puzzling, since they nearly always show up in the morning. In fact, those in our area are very punctual. They arrive between 8:30 and 9 a.m. and are gone by 10:30. If they take evening handouts, it's in somebody else's yard.

Birding experts say "evening" refers to the birds' colors—yellow, black, yellow-green, white—the shades of sunset.

The birds are migrants from the far north and west, and extremely rare visitors in this area until people began winter feeding 25 or 30 years ago. Now they arrive shortly after the orioles and tanagers depart in autumn, and they'll stay until about the time the warblers come back in April. During the bleak winter months, they are the biggest splash of color around. Cardinals may be more brilliant individually, but cardinals seldom travel in flocks, and nothing brightens a yard as quickly or as brightly as two dozen grosbeaks appearing as if by magic.

159

Their personalities are bright, too. Frigid temperatures and deep snow don't seem to bother them in the least. They take time, between mouthfuls of sunflower seeds, to twitter contentedly or happily gossip among themselves. As long as there is plenty to eat, why worry about the weather?

Unfortunately, they never stay long. Maybe they're just a bit restless. Maybe they're constantly looking for better handouts. And maybe they have a regular banquet circuit they must travel. Three meals here, then three on the next block, then four more at the farm along the river. Then back here for another round.

But getting on their circuit isn't easy. They're selective—make that finicky—and will bypass dozens of feeders for every one they visit. Why? Who knows? There seems little reason for anything the evening grosbeaks do.

In fact, with evening grosbeaks, the only thing you can count on is that they are not a bird to count on.

November stars

It happens each fall. When the leaves are down and the air is cleansed, the sky is rediscovered. All those stars.

Somehow, in summer, it's difficult to notice how obliterated the night sky can be. Sure, if you're camping on a mountaintop or have a cabin in some wilderness, you might have a clear view of the summer stars, but then the mosquitoes probably wouldn't let you sit out and look.

Now, however, with the roof of leaves gone and the dust of summer starting to be filtered out of the air, the starry nights are back. Already, the constellations of winter—the most easily recognized and best known—are parading across the sky each night. Astronomers usually consider January the best month for star-watching, when the sky is even clearer, but it's always so cold on those nights that you can't stay out for more than a few minutes. Now, it's still relatively comfortable out there if you bundle up.

You don't have to be an astronomer to learn the November and December star formations. There's Orion the Hunter and Pegasus the Winged Horse and Taurus the Bull and the Seven Sisters of the Pleiades. They were named by imaginative Greeks and Romans in ancient times, and it takes plenty of imagination to see a horse or bull or hunter up there. But look up these constellations in a book once and you should have no problem finding them on these starry nights.

Orion, in particular, stands out. Look for three stars in a line—the hunter's belt—low on the eastern horizon soon after dark. Following Orion across the sky is his faithful dog, Canis Major, with its brilliant star, Sirius. Above Orion is Taurus with its distinctive triangle of stars that are supposed to be the tips of the bull's horns and its nose. And still higher are the Pleiades, the dim cluster of stars that are called the Seven Sisters even though it's usually difficult to make out more than six. The Winged Horse is overhead, slightly to the south, and marked by a large, rather lopsided, square of four bright stars.

There are so many more formations to identify, too. Ursa

Major, the Great Bear, is usually known as the Big Dipper. Right now, it's standing on its handle on the northern horizon. With your eye, follow a line from the two bowl stars opposite the dipper's handle, and it will point to Polaris, the North Star, high overhead. And, while you're craning your neck to look nearly straight up, note a ragged W formation up there. That's Cassiopia, the Queen. And if you follow the dipper's handle through its bowl it will point out the Gemini, with its brilliant twins stars, Castor and Pollux.

Early risers actually have an advantage in seeing most of these formations. They are higher and shine brighter in the predawn hours.

Everyone can find that immense collection of stars called the Milky Way. As winter approaches, the Milky Way will become brighter, more spectacular, until it fairly dances and glitters in the frosty darkness.

In November the stars appear to hang low and friendly. At times you'll feel certain you could reach up and touch them if you could just climb some ridge. Walk in the woods at night, and look up through the naked limbs, and it appears the stars are attached to the branches themselves. They become gleaming baubles, making every huge maple and sycamore an exquisite Christmas tree.

For best star-gazing, pick a night when the moon is new or a mere sliver, so that it doesn't overwhelm the eye, and try to get away from the lights of civilization. A suburban backyard is many times better than, say, a city street. And a meadow or pasture is better still. The darker your surroundings, the brighter the stars.

Sure, it can be a little nippy out there at night, even now, but the star show can be worth the chill. And there are no mosquitoes.

Moment of magic

Have you noticed the difference? Have you noticed how striking the colors of twilight have become, how spectacular the sunsets are these days?

Twilight comes early now—too early for most of us not yet used to standard time—but it comes softly and gently. In mid-winter, the approach of darkness is sharp, cutting, often accompanied by piercing wind and snow or sleet.

Now, it slips down the hillsides in soft blue shadows and settles over the homes like a blanket, wrapping up the day in secure contentment. And, under certain conditions, twilight and sunset are the best times of the day.

Late-autumn skies normally contain plenty of clouds, particularly as the daylight fades, and those clouds move quickly, hurrying to escape the flames leaping at them from the vanishing sun. Watch the clouds in the minutes before sunset and they'll change colors half a dozen times in a twinkling. They'll be purple and violet green for an instant, then suddenly orange and crimson as the sunset's spreading wildfire catches them, flickers brilliantly, and almost immediately fizzles. It can be awesome.

One of the best spots for watching both the twilight and sunset is high on a wooded ridge above a pond. The smooth surface on the pond reflects, even magnifies, the color scheme above. You have to watch closely, but on those certain evenings the water is magically transformed. It is liquid rose for a moment, then acres of melted gold. Then it is gray water again, and you're not really certain you saw what you think you did.

Linger on the ridge for a while longer, and you can almost watch the twilight come. It will fill the hollows first, like floodwaters, and will crowd around the pond edges. Yet, the pond itself will hold its light longer, fading reluctantly from its shimmer to a soft glow to a cold blue aura.

Yet, when you climb down into the valley or the hollows, you'll find the twilight has lessened there a bit; in fact, it now seems darker up on the hill. It's an illusion, of course, one of many that late-autumn twilight creates.

Too often, people today fail to notice the evening sky. They're either battling traffic on their way home from work or are busy getting supper on the table or reading the evening paper or already planted in front of the television. But once countrymen knew this fascinating, and elusive, phenomenon well. They paused and watched at the end of a day spent cutting firewood, or glanced up while returning from the barn and the milking chores. They know the magical moment.

Our habits and routines have changed, and maybe that's a shame. The twilight show is still as delightful as ever.

A reminder and a promise

It is still hanging up there for all the world to see, abandoned and slightly tattered, but still serving a useful purpose. It is a reminder and a promise.

The oriole has been gone for months, and it won't be back for several more months, but its unique, expertly woven nest is still intact, up there swaying in the wind. It is a reminder of last summer and a promise that another spring and summer will, indeed, come around again.

And right now, as we approach the long, cold slope that must be climbed before orioles and wildflowers and turtles and butterflies return, such assurances are necessary.

The oriole nest is seldom seen during the summer, concealed as it is by a million leaves. But now the leaves are gone and the nest is highly visible, a gray pouch swinging from slender twigs high above the back lawn or the river or some country road.

Probably no other bird in our area possesses the engineering skill of the oriole. Instead of plastering together a bowl-like nest in a tree crotch, as the robin does, the female oriole patiently weaves an eight-inch pouch of plant fibers, hair, grasses, yarn and string near the top of the tallest tree around. It may take her more than a week to finish the task. The male doesn't have time to help— he's too busy singing.

It is that song, a loud, rippling, liquid tune that greets the morning, and the male's striking orange and black plumage that make the bird so treasured during the spring and summer. The oriole is a June morning all by itself, fresh and exciting brilliance of color and sweetness of sound.

Now, that gray, ghostly pouch of a nest is our reminder of that oriole. Sometimes, after months of listening to blue jays jeering and crows quarreling, it's hard to remember that some birds can sing.

Jays and crows, of course, don't desert us during the winter, as the oriole does, so maybe they deserve some credit. But one oriole is still worth a hundred jays or crows. It won't rob nests or kill other birds' babies, as jays and crows do, and it is so much better to look at and listen to. And jays and crows make sloppy nests in comparison with the oriole's masterpiece. No, a five-month absence may not be too high a price at all to pay for the oriole.

So, until that April or May dawn when the first oriole song comes wafting down from some tall tree, we'll have to be content with the birds of winter. There will be chickadees at the feeder and mockingbirds in the bushes and those jays and crows making their speeches and arguing over which is really lord of the woods.

But at least we have that old oriole nest to assure us that it won't always be this way. The oriole will return, and so will the tanager and the thrush and the swallow. Spring will be back. And now, with the height of winter looming ahead, that assurance is valuable indeed.

Thanksgiving with Gib

Every Thanksgiving Day I feel a little guilty if I spend the day watching TV football or hiking the hillside or visiting one of the city restaurants. It seems I should be buzzing wood.

Thanksgiving is a day for tradition, possible more so than any other holiday, Christmas included, and my family's traditional Thanksgiving activity was buzzing wood. That and hunting rabbits and having Gib over for dinner.

For those who grew up in all-electric homes or in houses heated with automatic furnaces, "buzzing wood" was our term for cutting the winter's supply of firewood. We would cut enough that day for the entire winter, and often had it all buzzed by noon, leaving the afternoon free for hunting rabbits.

We called it "buzzing" because that's the sound the saw made when it zipped through the logs. Bzzzzing! Bzzzzing! The saw belonged to Gib, a bachelor uncle of mine who lived on the next farm, and had a monstrous blade. At least it looked monstrous to a small boy like me.

Gib always operated the huge saw, which ran on a belt strung to his tractor. He fed the logs to the blade on the saw's movable table and my older brothers fed the logs to Gib as fast as they could. No sooner would the ring die away from one "bzzzzing" than another would begin. My job was keeping the pile of firewood under the saw from getting so high that it would interfere with Gib's smooth rhythm.

Thanksgiving Days always seemed so much colder in those days than they are now. We could usually count on the ground being frozen—which meant that the logs we had gathered for the previous three weeks would be frozen to it—and often there was snow over them.

But the project would go on as scheduled, regardless of the weather. Gib would drive his tractor to our farm shortly after dawn and we were expected to be out behind the woodshed waiting for him. He might say "How are you guys this morning," while setting up the saw and maybe "Looks like more snow com-

167

ing," while checking over the tractor. Then the sawdust started flying and he wouldn't say another word until noon.

By then the sawdust pile was three or four feet high but the mountain of firewood behind the shed was perhaps ten feet high and twenty feet across. It was time for dinner. And what a dinner it was—turkey, dressing, cranberry sauce, corn, green beans, mashed potatoes, gravy, homemade bread, pumpkin or apple pie, or both. The works. Just like most people have for supper on Thanksgiving. We always had ours at noon because our day's work was already finished.

I never thought about it at the time, but it must have been those dinners that made Gib so willing to head our buzzing operation. He probably didn't eat as much in a month as he got that day. The pile of empty cans of stew and fruit behind his house nearly matched our stack of firewood.

Gib was usually the only "guest" at dinner but just that one addition threw our carefully designed seating arrangement into chaos. The table was big, but with seven boys and six girls in the family, plus our parents, it was just long enough for elbow-to-elbow eating. The presence of Gib—and he was a mighty big man—usually pushed a couple of kids off the corners.

We knew better than to complain though, because Mom, who was Gib's "big sister" even though she barely reached his waist, always had a stock answer.

"If you have that much room in heaven you'll be lucky..."

After dinner, those who could move went out looking for rabbits while the others talked off the big meal. As for the firewood, it would take a week of working after school to get it all stacked inside the woodshed. But it would be another year, until next Thanksgiving, before we'd hear the "bzzzzzzing" again.

Freeze-up

The sun was already slipping behind the hill, even though it was still afternoon. It was red and bright, blazing through a cloudless sky, but there was little doubt now that it had lost its battle. Ice was coming.

For days, the sunshine had fought against the ice in the marsh's shallow water. This night, the ice would win out.

Before the sun was completely gone, tiny fringes of crystalline lacework began appearing around each of the weed stalks at the shore. The temperature was dropping steadily, and already the grass on the bank was stiffening, emitting an audible crunch when stepped on.

Still, it wasn't really much colder than the previous evenings. It was just that all the conditions were finally right for the freezing of the marsh. The sky had cleared, removing the clouds and mist that shielded the marsh. And the water had stopped churning. Not only was the wind gone, but the water itself had ceased the tumbling it does when one level is of perceptibly different temperature than another. Now it all had been sufficiently cooled. All was ready.

Evidently, the wild creatures knew what was happening. Juncos and chickadees that had been busy at the marsh on other afternoons did not appear. No jays or crows flew by or called from the woods. That evening, no raccoons stopped by. No opossums. No squirrels. The only activity noticed was by a whiskered muskrat, hurrying to its lodge with a bulrush root in its mouth. A pair of mallard ducks was on the water, but they floated in silence, contemplating the night ahead.

In the weedy backwaters, slivers of ice began reaching out from each plant, stretching fingers in every direction. In moments, the fingers met and welded, then pushed off toward others. Soon a transparent film covered the area, locking the weed stems in place, and continually edging farther out toward the open water.

As the pale, early winter moon climbed higher, sparkling sil-

169

ver crystals took shape in a thousand intricate designs at the base of the cattails and rushes in the deeper water. It was as if the cold was traveling down the weeds to the water. Again, as in the dense weed patches, the ice gradually stretched away from the cattails, leaving behind the streaks and lines and arrows that would highlight the ice sheet by dawn.

The ducks slept, their heads tucked under their wings, and the muskrat stayed in his lodge, secure in the knowledge that a freeze-up would make his reeds-and-mud den virtually impregnable from predators. And the ice continued creeping farther out, thickening as it went.

Before dawn, the ducks, with their expanse of open water dwindled to a circle no more than six feet across, flew off for more suitable winter quarters. The muskrat slept on, his breath leaving a rim of white frost around the air hole in his lodge. The sun's arrival found the little marsh silent and motionless. Ice was stretching from shore to shore. The battle was over.

Thoreau's apples

December usually isn't thought of as a time for wild fruit, but some of the most colorful berries of the year are ripe now. Most are a brilliant red, tiny, and last far into the winter. And most are far more suited to a partridge's taste than a person's.

Oh, a few late-autumn fruits are edible, such as the wild crabapples and the cranberries, but they're not quite what you'd pick by the handful just to pop into your mouth, like raspberries and blueberries.

Henry David Thoreau, however, was eloquent in his praise of the crabapples, which are easier to find now that the leaves are gone.

"To appreciate the wild and sharp flavors," said H.D., "it is necessary that you breathe the sharp autumn air. The outdoor air and exercise which the walker gets gives a different tone to his palate, and he craves a fruit which the sedentary would call harsh and crabbed. This noblest of fruits must be eaten in the fields, when your system is all aglow with exercise, when frosty weather nips your fingers, the wind rattles the bare boughs or rustles the few remaining leaves, and the jay is heard screaming around. What is sour in the house a bracing walk makes sweet. Some of these apples might be labeled, 'To be eaten in the wind.'"

Well, there is a wild crabapple tree beside one of my favorite trails, so occasionally I pick one as I pass. As Thoreau did, I nibble it as I walk, all aglow with exercise. I eat it in the wind, when frosty weather nips my fingers, when the few remaining leaves rustle, when a jay is screaming. But it's still far from sweet.

Cranberries, too, are a little tart when eaten right from the bog. But I go looking for them anyway at this time of year, just to maintain a link with some long-vanished farmers in my area.

As many farmers did a century ago, they had dammed a brook and created a little bog for their cranberries, perhaps as a cash crop or maybe just for their own use. But the farmers long ago moved on, and the land was abandoned. The dam rotted away, the brook returned to a single channel, and saplings and briars crept into the bog.

Still, the cranberry plants survived—after all this time I think of them as wild—and each fall I can find a few bright red berries down there. Apparently, only those plants bordering the brook itself bear fruit, so the harvest is small indeed, but as long as there are a few berries each year, the legacy of the old farm somehow remains intact.

The other red berries are mostly for the birds. One is even called partridgeberry, because of the way grouse gravitate toward it when times get rough. It is a tiny, ground-hugging plant with evergreen leaves that grows best in damp forests and sandy knolls.

Wintergreen, a similar, but unrelated plant—even though many woodsmen use names of it and the partridgeberry interchangeably—also produces minute red berries among its green mat of leaves, and also attract grouse, quail, wild turkeys and sometimes foxes and opossums.

Black alder berries are ruby-red right now, and the most easily found by the casual country wanderer. They stand out like beacons in the swamps, thick clusters of glowing berries on stark bushes as big as small trees.

Barberries are still around, too, particularly in fence rows or pastures on old farms. The oval, crimson fruit lures a number of birds and some animals, but people who have tasted it would have to be starving to munch it willingly. One of its other names is sourberry.

Frost ferns

There are a few times every winter—not many, mind you, but a few—when I resent these modern storm windows just a little. They have robbed us of some awesome frost formations.

Back in the old farmhouse where I grew up, the windows were framed with wood and were quite loose-fitting. They made for chilly dawns and cut deeply into the heating capacity of our wood stove, but they provided dazzling displays of hoarfrost almost every morning. Maybe that didn't quite make up for their inefficiency, but almost.

Ice still forms on the outside of metal storm windows, of course, but without the warmer air seeping out, the panes are simply coated uniformly. There's not much beauty in that.

When warmer air, particularly moist warm air, is allowed to escape in a trickle and then mixes with the freezing temperatures outside, the results are stunning. Intricate patterns develop, the kind they used to say were painted by Jack Frost. And they often do appear to have been painted, for the escaping air spreads and streaks across the glass as it condenses into delicate ice flakes, leaving markings that greatly resemble brush strokes.

Most of the time the designs, pretty as they are, defy description. But occasionally, a window will have a leak that lends itself to a particular formation. That's how it is on my bathroom window—it has a magnificent fern sculptured in ice outside it nearly every morning at this time of year.

Once in a while, though, the "leaves" of the fern will become a little too thick and will lose their straight lines for a more fuzzy appearance, and then it becomes a drooping goldenrod. Apparently, it has to do with how warm and how moist the air is when it hits the outside cold, for after somebody takes a hot shower on a cold night, the figure frequently "grows" into a tree with a full crown.

My only other window that develops good frost pictures is in the attached garage, which isn't as warm as the bathroom but is much damper, especially when the car is covered with snow when put away. That brings about a virtual forest on the row of windows, complete with underbrush, erect trunks, leafy canopies and even a cloud cover. Absolutely awesome.

The best time to view the frost formations, of course, is in the early mornings, just when the sunshine hits them. Then they sparkle and glitter as much as any Christmas tree ornament. For a little while. The same sunshine that enhances their brilliance so much will erase them before long. The ferns and goldenrods will wither into streaks and droplets of water, and perhaps finally into icicles.

But they'll be back next morning. If the bathroom window isn't air tight. Or the garage has melting snow inside. Or if the windows are the old-fashioned wooden kind that don't fit just right. A couple of times a year they would be worth having just for the frost. A couple of times a year.

Christmas greenery

The greens of Christmas can be—and should be—more than just decorations. They are symbols, reminders of what this season means both in the natural sense and the spiritual sense. Green means life.

Now, when the land lies stark and bleak, when most of the countryside is gripped in winter's icy grasp, the vibrant green of the pine and spruce, of the hemlock and holly, offers reassurance that all is not dead, that no winter lasts forever. There will be another spring, another season of rebirth and growth. When the temperature dips near zero and the fierce winds howl, we need such assurances.

Historians say the custom of bringing greens indoors in winter has been going on for centuries, even before that night in Bethlehem that brought about a new meaning to the greens. Back in the primitive times, those people saw in the pines and spruces the persistence of life during the darkness of winter, and how the evergreens represented hope for the future.

Since the Child of Bethlehem, the greens have taken on another meaning, a deeper meaning. They are symbols of a revived spiritual life, symbols of faith that the darkest times can be overcome, symbols of hope for better days ahead. The greens endure the harshest winters, should men and their beliefs do less?

So we choose a tree from the dozens stacked around parking lots, or cut our own after tagging one on some farmer's hillside, and decorate it with the festive lights and cherished old baubles. We bring in sprigs of hemlocks or cedar to drape across the doorways or fireplace mantels. We put wreaths of holly on the doors.

They are our source of encouragement, our link with the enduring things of the natural world. Evergreens were here before any other trees; in fact, they were here when the first men arrived upon this planet. They have survived all the winters of the ages, all the wars and plagues and famines the world has known.

And still they stand green and alive, ready to endure another winter. They again are helping us to remember and to believe, and perhaps understand in a small way, what faith is all about.

Winterberry

It's usually called a black alder, this wild shrub of the low-lands, but right now it's other name—winterberry—is more appropriate. It is carrying the season's greetings, a bright red greeting, in the outdoors.

Most of the countryside is a somber gray and brown now, awaiting snow, but the black alder is doing its best to brighten things up, decorating the stream banks and marshes with its brilliant, holly-like berries. Those berries seem unusually profusive, and maybe even a brighter red, this year. But they probably did last year, too. It's just hard to remember from one year to the next how delightful winterberries can be.

Black alders are not big or impressive, except in November and December. In fact, during the rest of the year, they are completely overwhelmed by surrounding bushes and trees. But their patience pays off. Now, long after the other trees have not only given up their fruits, but also have been stripped of their leaves, the black alders come into the spotlight.

Drive out through the country and you'll see them, the clusters of red berries standing out like beacons, glowing in the wetlands and waste places. Often, passersby will stop and snip a twig or two for indoor decorations—as they do with pussy willows in early spring—but they'll probably get their feet wet in doing so. Bushes with the thickest clusters and brightest berries always seem to grow closest to the water. However, it's a small price to pay for such a festive ornament.

The berries are heavy and pulpy, but not palatable to us. In fact, not even many birds eat them, which may explain why they remain so long after the other wild fruits have vanished. When times get tough, when snow lies deep and ice locks away the low-lying seeds, some birds and mice and squirrels will be forced to collect these wild rubies. Until then, they're just for looks.

Now, while the forest floor is still uncovered by snow, you might be able to find another kind of winter fruit, the partridge-berry. It's a trailing vine, seemingly fragile, that can form a virtual carpet in the open woods and clearings. Its berries, too, are bright red. They're far smaller than the black alder's, and you have to be almost on top of them to even notice them. But the birds know where they are, and in many places have already harvested all the fruit.

There are some bittersweet berries left, clinging to their vines on the fencerows and gnarled, old trees. Bittersweet also is sometimes brought indoors to spruce up a wreath or to be dangled from a mantel, but beside the black alder berries, the bittersweets look pale and lifeless.

So it is to the black alder that countrymen look when they need a bit of color in a time of year that can be bleak. And now, with Christmas approaching, the lowly bush with the scarlet berries takes on special significance. Each one, in its own way, is a Christmas tree.

Snow light

December nights—or any nights in winter, for that matter—aren't really dark at all. Not when there is snow on the ground.

Stars and the moon are not necessary, either, although both add immeasurably to the delight of a late-night walk. But even on starless and moonless nights, the snow's strange luminescence makes walking without flashlights or lanterns not only possible but preferable. In the woods, the paths become enchanting avenues, bounded by the stark outlines of tree trunks. Bushes become vague mounds of blackness. In fact, trails seem to be defined more clearly at night than they are in the harsh light of day.

The key is to let our eyes get accustomed to the night, accept the shadowless countryside on its own terms. Once we leave the glare of homes and windows and street lights behind, we can enter a world far removed from what we notice during daylight hours. It's a world of silence, both soothing and strangely exciting. The only sounds, aside from the occasional yip of some distant fox or the call of an owl up on the hillside, are our own footsteps in the snow.

We'll notice, however, that it is a world without color. Everything is black or white. Night vision supposedly lacks some color sensitivity but it accentuates contrasts. At night, it is not difficult to identify objects strictly by shapes.

A few nights after last year's first snow—first snows are always irresistible, but this year's storm was almost too much—daughter Sandy joined me and Rusty, our golden retriever, on our before-bed stroll. Rusty and I go out often, but it was a first for Sandy. I told her the flashlight wasn't necessay, but I don't think she believed me until we were a hundred yards away from the house. Then, the soft, natural glow of the snow took over.

We followed the stream, then crossed a footbridge, climbed a gentle slope and entered the pine grove. That convinced her. Even in the dense pines, without benefit of the moon or stars, the snow provided enough light that we could follow Rusty's tracks as he wound his way through the forest.

Sometimes, there are other creatures afoot at night. Rusty often chases rabbits and dives into the snow after mice. We have come across raccoons at the creek. We have seen owls swoop low through the woods. We've seen grouse parading through the brush. And, in those times before the dog arrived, we once came face to face with one of those foxes as it explored the meadow. The night is their time for activity, their time to search for supper. They're all out and about in summer, too, but seeing them then is practically impossible.

However, owls and foxes, as pleasant as they are to find, are only fringe benefits of walks in the snow. The night itself, with its magical aura of freshness and quiet sublety, can awake new senses and new values. Add the snow, and there is, indeed, a whole new world revealed.

Cutting our tree

Thanks to a note in a greeting card, a friend's generosity, and a little bit of magic, our Christmas has an extra touch of nostalgia this year. It had been years since we tried the old custom of searching the woods for our tree.

Several years ago we decided scrounging around nurseries and supermarket lots for a "live" tree wasn't worth the effort, so we bought one of the artificials. It was just as green, shaped better, and reusable, we told ourselves, so why bother with the real thing? Besides, there would soon be a shortage of trees, and this would be our little bit for conservation.

But now we know we were cheating ourselves all this time. We went out and cut our own tree over the weekend, and it might just have been the highlight of our season—at least until the kids start attacking the presents on Christmas morning.

It isn't that we had never done it before. It's just that the senses had forgotten what it is like, and what is more pleasant than reawakening old memories? Cutting a tree yourself offers rewards impossible to gain by buying a tree off the rack.

It has a sound, smell and feel all its own. And all the benefits are enhanced a hundredfold when the man doing the chopping is surrounded by excited children who have never seen it done before.

The offer to come out and cut the tree was unexpected, but as soon as we read it in the Christmas card, we jumped at the chance. Had the note not been included, we probably would have used the plastic tree again, and never would have known Sunday's magic.

We went right out to our friend's woods and started looking. The trees were beautiful—white pine, white spruce, blue spruce, hemlock—scattered all around in a hundred sizes and shapes.

Almost immediately, we realized a shortcoming in these modern, low-ceilinged houses. All the best trees were far too tall for us, and of course, getting a smaller one that would appeal to the kids would be virtually impossible. Each had his favorite, and yells of "Daddy, this one is just right" and "No, not that one" came from all sides.

Finally, an eight-foot white spruce was chosen—even though it would have to be trimmed to seven feet later—and I set upon it with the axe. I like swinging an axe anyway, and in seconds the "whack, whack" sound and the smell of the newly cut wood got to me. It was like the old days again—and I loved every minute of it. The kids, watching just out of reach of the flying chips, applauded and screamed "Timberrr!" in unison when the tree toppled.

We picked it up, all four kids—Suzy, Sandy, Steve and Scott—and I, staining our hands with the aromatic pitch in the process (something we had never done from a supermarket tree) and started back toward the car. That's when the rest of the magic appeared.

Tiny flakes of snow, the first of the year, started drifting down upon us. It's timing was incredible. It sparked a loud rendition of Jingle Bells that made up for its lack of harmony with uninhibited enthusiasm. It made me wish we really had a one-horse open sleigh with which to carry the tree home.

Maybe we'll work on that for next year. But whether we find a sleigh or not, we know where we'll get our tree. If our friend doesn't mind a woods full of noise.

Clocks and calendars

For those who live by clocks and calendars—and that includes nearly all of us these days—one year will end this weekend and another will begin. But what is really ending? What is beginning?

The few people who still live close to the land, those who listen to the chimes of a natural clock, know that New Year's Day actually arrives on that morning in late March when the first redwinged blackbird appears, or that day in April when the fields finally are fit for plowing, or perhaps that drizzly evening when the first chants of the tiny tree frogs echo from the marshes.

But Jan. 1? That's a line of demarcation drawn up by men who seem to need beginnings and endings. Maybe it's for reaching conclusions, for tallying up our achievements for the 12-month period. We want scorecards; was 1983 better than 1982?

The natural year, obviously, has no beginning and no end. It's an endless cycle. Seeds sprout, grow, bloom, ripen and produce new seeds.

Right now they are at rest, but dormancy is not death. Look at the twigs of your backyard bushes—lilacs or rhododendrons or dogwoods—and you can already see the promise of spring in the buds. They didn't wait until a New Year's Day to form; in the natural world, tomorrow is always part of today.

It's the same with the animals. The insects that perished in the frost of last October had earlier deposited their eggs, insuring their return in another summer.

Some of the ducks on the pond are already starting courtship rituals. Owls will be nesting in a couple of weeks. Deer hiding in the hemlock groves may already be carrying their fetal fawns.

The calendar does serve a purpose for those who merely endure winter. We can mark off the days, knowing that when January and February are gone, we'll almost have winter licked.

We've been through it enough times. All we have to do is remind ourselves that there are just as many springs as winters. We *know* winter will not last forever.

185

However, the chickadee in the forest cannot know as much. Next week is no new year for him; it's just a continuation of his struggle to survive.

The woodchuck snoozing in his burrow, and the frogs and turtles buried beneath the frozen ponds, are not checking off dates on calendars. Instinct told them when to sleep; temperature will tell them when to wake.

Temperature and light—and time—govern all creatures but men. Only men try to divide time into neat little packages. Seconds, minutes and hours. Days and weeks. Spring and summer. Fall and winter.

Only men will be starting something new at midnight tomorrow. The rest of the world will just keep rolling, around and around.

Snow walk

It's an ideal day for a winter walk. Fresh snow on the ground. Light snow falling. Only moderately cold, about 20 degrees. Cold enough to be invigorating, not cold enough to be painful.

As always, I'm surprised by how many rabbit tracks I find in the meadow and the brushy thicket beyond the yard. I see rabbits once in a while, but tracks prove there must be dozens running around back there at night.

Water in the stream looks black against the white background. Stream is high, nearly up to the bridge. Icy fringes. Very pretty.

I hear crows making a ruckus in the trees, and I correctly guess the reason. They're badgering a huge owl, which is roosting halfway up a big pine. Despite all the noise, the owl seems unconcerned. It watches as we walk almost beneath it, and it's still sitting there, out in the open, ignoring the crows, as we pass.

We try to cross the bog and find, because of the high water, we can't jump the brooks as usual. Rusty won't cross the first brook on a rotting old log until I demonstrate. Later, I cross another rushing brook on a fallen tree, about four feet above the water. That's not for Rusty. He wades through.

We wander toward the river, first swinging around a small pond so I can check the tall pine where I saw two raccoons snoozing in the sunshine in October. I saw them only that one time, but I check that tree—and most similar trees—every time I pass now.

There is too much snow on the pond ice for skating, but it's smooth—water was high enough to cover all the lily pads this time. My kids learned to skate on this pond, but in recent years the lily pads and other weeds have increased so much they hamper skating a great deal. But the ice gives me a chance to check a wood duck house—it's empty—and poke about briefly in the cattails, looking for muskrat lodges. But I don't trust the ice back there enough for thorough investigation. I've broken through too many times, and it would be a long, cold run back to the house. I glance up just in time to see a rabbit loping along the shore. Rusty is with me and doesn't see it. In an instant, the rabbit is gone. Just one more set of tracks.

There are a few mallards in an open section of the river, where the stream joins it. They're running out of open water; most of the river is frozen. I'm not about to try that ice yet, however. Rusty is already having ice problems, with it packing between pads in his paws. One pad is bleeding, I whistle him over and break out the ice, a task I'll have to perform many times on this walk. I think of how much trouble he had with his tender paws last winter. Maybe Bettie should have made him booties, as she suggested.

We walk along the river and find fox tracks. They're rather faint; probably made early last night. I'm eager to see the snow in the evergreen grove, so we climb the steep, rocky hill. It's exhausting, and a bit dangerous, because some of the rocks are coated with ice, but the ridge is beautiful. The grove looked dark and brooding from the river, but up close the green is fresh and vibrant. The feathery hemlock branches in particular are lovely with their lacing of spotless snow.

Fresh squirrel tracks run between some trees and mouse tracks—or some insomniac chipmunk's—dot the stone walls. This woods sometimes seems deserted by animals when I visit in summer, so it's good to have the tracks to assure me they're still up there. We pause to peer into a small cave in a rocky ledge, hoping to find a fox curled up there. Never have, but I always check it out, ever since we found a dead one lying in a similar crevice a few miles away. Don't know why foxes are never there; it looks like the perfect place. I'd use it if I were a fox.

The spring that starts what we call Tumbledown Brook is still open and bubbling, but icy around the edges and a little more sluggish than usual. We wander along the ridge to a ledge where the boys sometimes camp in summer. Last time I walked up there in snow, I found tracks that showed a fox had trotted into camp, sniffed around their makeshift stone fireplace, and moved on. This time it's a squirrel trail. Wonder if those animals visit when the boys have their tent up.

Along an old truck lane, I find snowed-over jeep tracks, probably from yesterday, and a dog's track on top of them. I remember the lean and mean coon dog Rusty and I ran into up there last fall. Does Rusty? He wanted no part of that fellow, and

I don't blame him. Is that beast still around?

We cross a clearing, noting numerous rabbit and mouse tracks, and start down the far slope. The snow seems to be increasing, but I think much of it is just being shaken loose from the trees. Little ground pines on the trail are enchanting, each one with its cap of snow. They do, indeed, look like miniature pines and I feel like a giant as I carefully step over them.

We find tracks of a grouse—we always find grouse in that area—and follow them as they cross my trail, then zig-zag through the brush for a hundred feet or so. They lead to a small knoll, then vanish. There are no signs of a struggle, so the bird apparently flew off, rather than being carried off.

The trail winds back to another clearing, where I pick up a fairly fresh fox track. It's headed in a different direction than I want to go, so I backtrack it, trying to see where it spent the earlier snowfall. The dainty, single-file prints—which make Rusty's look big and clumsy in comparison—follow a motorcycle trail for some distance, then wander through the woods for a while, then join a narrow lane near a hemlock grove. In the past, we've found spots where foxes have waited out storms curled up beneath low-hanging hemlocks. Today's tracks skirt the grove, however, and start down toward the river. I'm not ready to climb down yet, though, so I leave the fox and circle through the woods and reach the river half a mile upstream.

While still halfway up the slope, I see and hear a flock of crows harassing a bird out over the ice. The victim doesn't appear large enough to be the owl I saw earlier. Probably a hawk. Nothing is safe from the crows today.

Rusty's tracks are still showing a bit of blood, but he's as eager as ever. For every mile I walk, he must cover at least two. It's only when he realizes we're heading home that he starts losing his enthusiasm. Today it's when we reach the first paved road. Suddenly, he's tired and trots along behind instead of dashing on ahead.

It's snowing harder now, and the snow is blowing into our faces as we near home. Cars zoom by us. A mockingbird and a blue jay fly over the street. There are house finches and pigeons in the yards. We're back in "civilization." The owl and the fox and the grouse seem far away now, but we know they're not. Not far at all.

Ol'Icy Fingers

It dawned on me the other morning—one of those below-zero mornings—that I'm getting soft. What would Betsy and Daisy and Beauty and Pansy think if they could see me now?

I had driven to work, being exposed to the frigid air only as long as it took to leap out of the car, close the garage door and leap back in, and later to walk a block from the parking lot to the office. Not even five minutes outside.

Yet, when I got back inside, I complained that my hands were so cold they hurt, and I remember thinking how glad I was that I didn't have to work outdoors on a morning like that.

Then I remembered Betsy and Daisy and the rest. They were among the cows on our farm, the cows I was milking by hand every morning just a few years ago. No wonder they grumbled when they saw me stomp through the snow to the barn.

"Here comes ol' Icy Fingers again."

But I never minded the milking, once I had forced myself out of bed. There was no heat in the barn, of course—in fact, the cracks in the siding were so wide there would be almost as much snow inside as out—but it still beat the other chores, like breaking ice in the various water troughs, throwing down hay and feeding and watering the chickens.

I never could stand working with chickens. They're too stupid. At least cows can be trained a little; you know, to come when called, to go into the right stalls as soon as I opened the gates, and to stand relatively still while I take the milk. Except for Beauty; she loved to kick over the bucket when it was just about filled.

For the most part, though, the cows and I got along just fine. As soon as I stepped inside the barn and snapped on the lights, they'd start moving toward the milking stalls, huge breath clouds billowing out with every snort. They didn't seem to mind the cold, so why should I?

Since I never figured out how to milk with gloves on, I always peeled them off and put them on the overturned five-gallon bucket that served as my stool—so that at least part of me would benefit from them—and start right in. Inevitably, at the first touch, a monumentous shudder crackled through the cow. Then, we both warmed, literally, to the task.

I prided myself on being able to withstand the cold in those days. By the time I got back to the house, the younger kids were just getting up for school. They'd come tumbling down the stairs, with half their clothes on and carrying the other half, so they could crowd around the kitchen stove. Always, their feet were still bare. It was too cold upstairs to waste time putting shoes on.

As they danced from one foot to the other, trying to keep both off the cold linoleum, I'd laugh at them.

"What are you going to do when winter comes?" I'd ask. They were too busy shivering to answer.

Now, I drive to an office instead of plowing through snow-drifts to a barn. I sit on a cushioned chair instead of a cold bucket cushioned only with my gloves. And I'm behind a desk, not beside a cow.

But now the cold gets to me. My hands hurt. I really am getting soft.

I ought to do something about it. Maybe there's room at my place for a barn. I don't think Beauty would mind living in New England.

Beach in winter

The wind is sharp. Yes, there's always the wind.

And it's cold out there, no matter how bright the sunshine and how clear the sky.

But still, the lure is irresistible. The lonely expanses of sand and the invigorating salt air and the crashing waves beckon. Let others swarm to the beaches in summer, I'll take the winter.

There is a special appeal to the seashore now. All of its elements—the waves, the wind, the birds, even the beaches themselves—take on an intriguing new aura of primal wildness, an almost majestic sense of might.

Pick a spot where there are ancient rock formations at the water's edge—say, Beavertail Park on Jamestown—and watch the waves crash ashore. The foaming fury, the white spray, the rhythmic roar. It's awesome. The sights and sounds of the ages.

Or visit a busier place, maybe Galilee, and notice the difference from a trip in summer. In winter, the screaming is done by gulls, not children, and those fishermen heading out the channel do so because it is their livelihood, not a day-off lark. And if you stand in the winter wind and watch them, you'll gain a new respect for those men working out in the boats.

Stop by any open beach. Gone are the markings of summer. The traffic jams, the sun-worshipping crowds, the mazes of blankets and suntan lotions and transistor radios and plastic buckets and soda cans.

Now the beaches seem to have regained a measure of dignity. Once again, the sands are trackless, save for the prints of a few gulls and maybe a jogger or two. The tides leave a smooth, rippled design, depositing seaweed and bits of crab and mollusk shells instead of gum wrappers and cigarettes. Winter gives the sea a chance to reclaim the beaches for its own. Once more, man is merely a visitor; not a dominant squatter.

Perhaps half of the people you run into along the beaches now are birders, and they don't mind fierce weather. The other people—beachcombers with metal detectors, joggers, photographers and casual strollers—prefer sunshine and blue skies, but birders feel they can't lose, regardless of the weather.

If it's clear and relatively calm, they can see huge flocks of mergansers and migrating ducks just off shore, plus loons and grebes and all sorts of gulls. If it's stormy, the ocean birds will come in closer, the eiders and petrels and kittiwakes and gannets. Some ride the angry winds, others float calmly on the mountainous swells. They don't mind at all.

But the birds are really only a bonus. It is the shore, the beach itself that is the draw. It is the black ice on the rocks, the swaying dune grass, the whispering in the tall reeds. It is the gleam of the sunshine off the churning surf. It is that abandoned, and inviting, stretch of sand. It's a new frontier, challenging and intriguing and downright spectacular.

Even in the cold wind.

Ice fishermen

It takes a special kind of person to be an ice fisherman. He might be the *real* outdoorsman. Anybody can sit in the sunshine and cast for bass in May and June; it's something else to stand around in the January wind and wait for a pickerel to approach a line dangling through a hole in the ice.

Actually, ice fishermen are a little nutty, and they're proud of it. They chop holes in thick ice, set out little tip-up contraptions that signal strikes, and then wait around for something to happen. Out there on the frozen ponds. In the snow. In the wind. Brrrr!

It's not for me—my feet always get too cold—but I enjoy visiting these fishermen occasionally, just to listen to them.

A couple of old-timers I met on the ice recently were talking about raccoon hunting, and the comparable virtues of various coon dogs, and the price of coon, fox and muskrat pelts. How many summertime fishermen would know what running a pack of coon hounds is all about? They might know about motor boats and maybe they can tie flies and fill their creels on opening day of trout season, but somehow I think the old-fashioned outdoorsmen, the coon hunters and fox trappers, and ice fishermen, are a little more in tune with the woods and water and nature itself.

They obviously appreciate the outdoors a great deal to be there instead of in front of a TV set in some cozy living room, and sometimes it seems the perch or pike they might catch are only incidental. They're taking winter on its own terms, and becoming part of it. They hear the ice groan as the freeze deepens. They notice a crow screaming in the silent woods. They can tell by the sky if more snow is coming. They pause to look at the dark weeds undulating slowly in the water beneath the ice.

Oh, sure, they like to catch fish. They'll trudge around the pond, looking for the right spots, trying various coves and channels. That's part of the reason for the constant visiting that goes on between ice fishermen. They have to see if the other guy is doing better. Maybe he's found a school of fat yellow perch; maybe there's room for a couple of more tilts.

197

But it's obvious, too, that most of these fishermen just enjoy talking. They'll retell the story of that huge pike they pulled through the ice 20 years ago, and they talk about the time they had to drill through three feet of ice. They discuss their favorite baits and lures, and often the conversation wanders off into other fields, usually other phases of outdoors activity.

Most will say keeping warm is not such a big problem. They're prepared for the cold. Insulated underwear. Insulated boots. Heavy woolens. Parkas and hats and gloves. Hot coffee, and something stronger, for the insides. Chiseling the holes and roaming around and talking help, too. The loners, those who just sit and wait, are the ones who feel the cold most.

Ice fishermen may not be any more successful on catches-per-trip than their warm-weather counterparts, but one big pike hauled through the ice has to be a triumph surpassing half a dozen bass on some balmy spring day. The fact that these sportsmen are more sociable, and less competitive, perhaps shows their greater enjoyment of days away from the house.

Along with the fish, of course, they're gathering more tales to polish and pass on in the future. After all, isn't that one of the more important aspects of fishing?

All business

There is a rollicking, noisy band of birds wandering through nearly every woods in winter. They're bold, bouncy and boisterous. All except one member; one is all business.

Chickadees dominate the group, both in numbers and exuberance. They seem cheerful even in a snowstorm. Nuthatches are along, too, and titmice and downy woodpeckers, and occasionally a kinglet or two. You might find them separately, but many times they travel together, roaming about as if blown by the wind. All have a jauntiness, either in spirit or color or both, that defies the bleakness of the winter countryside.

But there is another member of those flocks, a bird that seldom is noticed. It's as drab as its name—brown creeper—and as somber as the season. However, it just might be the most important member of the gang.

Chickadees and their friends are never too busy to greet visitors to their domain. They're so nosy they have to investigate everything that happens in the woods, whether it be a man cutting firewood or a dog chasing a rabbit.

Nuthatches are the woods jesters even without trying. For one thing, they hunt for their meals by crawling down tree trunks—headfirst. For another, they're short and fat. Their bills are too long and their tails too short. But they're the faithful companions of the chickadees, adding their tuneless *yark, yark, yark* call to the chickadees' more pleasing *dee, dee, dee.*

Titmice, the gray-suited, crested southerners that are becoming more common all the time, are not as colorful or as noisy, although they call out frequently. Woodpeckers, of course, are a striking black and white, and the males add a dash of red on the head. Kinglets are tiny, olive-green bundles of enegry that, unfortunately, seem to be decreasing. The two varieties are called ruby-crowned and golden-crowned, and catching sight of these handsome little birds can highlight any stroll through the woods.

But who notices the creeper? All it ever seems to do is work. It flies to the bottom of a tree trunk and creeps upward while inspecting every inch of bark for grubs and insect larvae. When it's high in the tree, it swoops down to the bottom of another trunk and starts all over. No flashy crowns. No sassy calls. No acrobatics. No jackhammer drilling.

The creeper's life appears so humdrum. All work and no play. It seems strange that it would want to pal around with the carefree chickadee gang, and why would the chickadees and nuthatches want such a dull, party-pooper type tagging along?

Well, maybe it's the other way around. Maybe all the others are following the creeper, knowing that its industrious, systematic searching will provide enough goodies for everybody.

Maybe that's why the chickadees can afford to be cute, bouncing around as if January is as easy as July. Why should they worry about finding food? The brown creeper is there to do all the work.

The woods road

It's like a window on the world. No, it's more than that; it's a road into the world, the world of grouse and foxes and deermice and squirrels.

Once the road linked two rural villages. Barely wide enough for a wagon, it wound up and over a steep hill, skirting hollows, crossing ridges, sweeping around ledges, bouncing over boulders. It must have been a bumpy ride indeed.

But then, decades ago, a paved road was built a short distance away, and the lane was all but forgotten. Oh, motorcyclists still use part of it in summer and snowmobiles roar up it in winter, keeping it relatively clear of the ever-encroaching forest. They go as far as the hill's summit, then turn onto a newer lane that runs beneath power lines. On the far side of the hill, the ancient road was abandoned entirely.

Most of the cyclists and snowmobilers probably don't even know the road continues on that side. Bushes at the edge of the power-line clearing long ago obliterated the entrance, and in summer there is now a solid layer of leaves hiding the old ruts. Further back, trees have sprouted where wagons once rumbled. Some of those trees are 25 or 30 feet tall and eight to 10 inches thick. In summer, when saplings crowd in on every side, it's hard to tell there ever was a road on that slope. Now, however, the lane is again revealed and the snow shows that it's still in use—on both slopes—every night.

Foxes trot along every section of it, roaming off frequently, but always coming back. There are rabbit tracks galore, and occasionally the tracks of a grouse as it crosses from one cedar thicket to another. Squirrels and deermice travel on the old road, too, and maybe that's why the foxes like it so much. Judging from the amount of tracks, the traffic must be rather steady all night. And it's probably heavier yet in summer, when raccoons and skunks and opossums are more active than now.

The forest on the far side is mostly conifers—pines, hemlocks and cedars—with some tangled junipers inside areas

201

guarded by tumble-down stone walls. They probably were pastures at one time. On the near side, the far more rocky slope, there are dogwoods and birch near the bottom, then nearly all oaks as the road weaves its way toward the top.

Nowhere does the road go more than a few hundred feet without turning, and nowhere is it flat for even that long. Whoever carved that road into the hillside put out an immense effort.

There is a picturesque stone bridge over a brook, which is a work of art with hundreds of meticulously fitted rocks topped with huge, flat stones.

I walk the old road in all seasons, but it is in winter when I can really appreciate what it must have meant to the area's residents all those years ago. I wonder whether the snowmobilers realize the importance of that road. Somehow, it seems the foxes and squirrels do.

The rollicking otters

By this time of winter, the prolonged cold and deep snow often make life difficult for the wild creatures. Most of them are struggling just to survive. But not the otters; they're having a ball.

Foxes have to wander many miles each night to find a meal, and rabbits have to work just as hard to avoid being that meal, but the happy-go-lucky otters spend their time tobogganing down snowy riverbanks and playing follow-the-leader, popping in and out of holes in the ice.

Otters, once virtually exterminated in Rhode Island, have made a dramatic comeback and now it's possible to find them—or at least signs of them—on numerous ponds and rivers. They're more active during daylight hours than most mammals, but catching more than a glimpse of them is not easy. They are extremely wary and immediately vanish into the water and beneath the ice at the slightest sound or unexpected movement.

We lucked out recently, however, coming upon four adults—each about four feet long—frolicking in a stretch of open water where a stream tumbled into a pond. A couple of days later, we checked again and this time a young one, perhaps half-grown, was sunning itself on a rock, contentedly soaking up the rays as if it were June. It was below zero that morning.

Usually, though, it is the tracks that give away the otters. In deep snow, their short legs and webbed feet, which make them master swimmers, force them to plow through the snow rather than step over it. The trail is often a continuous trough, about eight or 10 inches wide.

Otters, of course, can't resist sliding. In summer, they create mud slides on steep banks. In winter, they slide through the snow. Even on a flat surface, such as pond ice, they'll run a few steps and then plunge ahead on their bellies, with their legs pulled back alongside the bodies. In loose snow, they can coast 15 feet or more on ice, and much longer distances down hillsides.

When they find an ideal slope, preferably one that ends with open water, they delight in it like children out of school for the day. They'll take turns sliding down into the water, climbing back up and doing it all over again and again. Their wet bodies continually make the path icier, and the trips get faster and faster. It looks like great fun.

Tracks over the frozen ponds also show another of their just-for-fun traits. Frequently, they interrupt their travels and roll around in the snow, for no reason except that it feels good. They've been known to float through small rapids, too, skillfully maneuvering past rocks like expert canoeists. Apparently, winter is one game after another if you're an otter.

Life has definitely gotten easier for otters now that trapping pressure has eased almost to the point of disappearing altogether. Their sleek, luxurious fur, which makes them impervious to the frigid water, once was sought almost as eagerly as the beaver's, and their numbers dwindled accordingly.

They also were persecuted to a lesser degree by some fishermen, who resented the amount of fish consumed by these agile acrobats, but recent studies have shown that otters normally take the slower-swimming "trash fish," such as crappies and suckers, rather than such sport fish as trout.

Now the otters are back.

Quietly, secretively, they returned to the ponds. They're still eating fish, but chances are we would never know they were around if they could resist playing in the snow. But that would be asking too much. Winter is fun time.

Lucky

Lucky must be sleeping in the barn, I thought. Why else would my old dog not respond to my whistling, particularly when it was suppertime? But he wasn't in the barn.

Nor could I find him anywhere else around the farm. When he didn't show up by the next evening, I started contacting the neighbors and driving the country roads. For more than a week, I searched for Lucky, but I never found a trace of my old friend.

That was many years ago, and at the time, I couldn't understand it. He must have been hit by a car, or been stolen, or been caught in some kid's raccoon trap. I refused to consider the possibility that he left by choice.

Apparently, I never will learn what became of Lucky, but now I've developed a new theory that soothes the painful memory of his loss. Actually, there are two theories, and to me, both are happy endings to his story.

Lucky was one of those all-American breeds, his ancestry totally indistinguishable after generations of dilution. But he was a champion pedigree when it came to serving as a kid's companion. We had a houseful of children, but I always thought of Lucky as "my" dog. I'm sure Larry and Herb and Judy and the others did likewise.

He was born, there in the barn, when I was maybe 10 or 11. He was the spunkiest, the most active of the puppies, and therefore was the one we chose when Dad said we could keep only one. Hence the name Lucky. His mother, Trixie, a wandering "wild" dog we had tamed a year or two earlier, also was disposed of at the same time.

So Lucky had only us, and he put his heart and soul into his role. As a pup, he was right at my heels, even when so young and small he couldn't get through the hayfields or tall grass in the woods without help. Later, he was to romp far ahead of me on these walks.

He learned to help me bring in the cows for milking. He knew what it meant when I came out of the house with a shotgun,

205

and he nearly bursts in anticipation of a day hunting rabbits. He ran along so often when I bicycled to town on errands that he knew the routine perfectly, trotting ahead from the hardware store to the grocery to the little shop where I bought ice cream cones to eat on the ride back.

Lucky loved playing in the snow and swimming in the creek and scaring the chickens and teasing the cats. Every afternoon when I got off the school bus, he'd be waiting at the road, and we'd race up to the house. He always won.

But, eventually, I grew up. My romps in the snow gave way to basketball games with my friends. I deserted the bike for a car, and Lucky couldn't keep up, although he tried for a while. Instead of taking him hunting on Saturdays, I used the time to wash my car so it would look good for my date that night.

Finally, I was out of school and working, being gone virtually from dawn to dark. My younger brothers were away at college. Judy was in high school, and like the rest of us, she had outgrown playing with a dog.

Lucky, too, was older, but he still had too much pup in him to retire to a sleeping spot in the sun. Mom remembers seeing him, all alone, rolling in the snow as we did with him years earlier. He still ran to the road when the yellow school bus rumbled into view. He still got excited when Dad put on his boots, because boots used to mean Larry or I was planning another venture into the woods.

But we didn't go with him anymore, and one day he disappeared. Maybe he really was stolen or hit by a car. However, I like to think he either reverted to the ways of his mother and lived out his life as a happy wanderer or found another farm where there were young children to play with, and run with, and share adventures with.

Maybe it never happened. It probably didn't. But I'm going to go on thinking it did.

A token of thanks

The idea came late last fall. We had a chance to help the bluebirds, and to say thanks for a summer of their company at the same time.

So, last weekend, on one of those days that seemed like early April, we walked back to the abandoned pasture to decide just where we'd put the birdhouses. And we found three bluebirds already there.

Now, bluebirds are among the earlier migrants, but they don't return before mid-February. No, these three birds must have wintered here, retreating to the cedar thickets during the most severe weather and existing on weed seeds.

They don't even look like bluebirds right now. In spring and summer, they are one of the most colorful, beautiful of our birds, with robin-like red breasts setting off bright blue bodies. At this time of year, they have rather drab, grayish backs and pale, washed-out orange breasts. We wouldn't have given them a second glance if it were not for their tails, still that unmistakable blue, the color of the sky in June.

Bluebirds have been dwindling in New England for several decades. Pesticides, competition from more aggressive birds and a decrease in farms and orchards are usually blamed for the decline. Bluebirds like living near orchards, hayfields, pastures and meadows, but they nest in hollow limbs. The few remaining places like that are usually taken over by starlings and house sparrows. The bluebirds simply are crowded out.

Last spring, we noticed a pair of bluebirds roaming around the edges of the old pasture. We hoped they would stay, but we were not too optimistic. Other bluebirds had stopped by in other springs, but always moved on before nesting time. We considered putting up a birdhouse then, but bluebirds can be rather finicky and we feared a house that suddenly appears in their midst would scare them off.

They must have found other accommodations, however, because we saw them occasionally through the summer. Not wanting to disturb them, we visited the pasture only a few times until after nesting season, so we never discovered where they nested, but just having them as neighbors was enough. We didn't get to hear their songs very often but we saw that blue—by comparison, a blue jay looks almost gray.

All through August and September, the bluebirds' family of five remained. They would be down in the tangle of weeds and would fly up to the fence posts upon our arrival. We kept expecting to find the place deserted, but the birds seemed reluctant to leave. Then, one day in late October, we strolled out there, and saw a whole flock of bluebirds—18 of them!—in the trees at the edge of the field. We had not seen that many in 10 years.

Two days later, they were gone, and the idea for several birdhouses around the place was formed. On a very un-bluebird-like day in December, the houses were built. We delayed putting them up because we didn't want starlings to claim them before bluebirds even saw them.

Now we have found that they apparently have been around all along. So the houses went up this week. We hope to lure the birds back for another season, of course, but it's also a way of re-paying them—saying thanks—for what they gave us last year.

The one-winged dove

The call came from somewhere on the hill—a haunting, almost plaintive, call. *Oooha, ooo ooo ooo.* Low, long, drawn-out. I wonder if that's my dove? Maybe it survived the winter after all. The call is a courting chant, but it sounds of sadness—was any bird ever more appropriately named than the mourning dove? Other birds sing, the doves moan.

This time, however, the call was most welcome. Odds are against it, of course, but I'm hoping it was the dove I found up there last fall. The dove with one wing.

It was on one of those crisp, sparkling October mornings that almost demanded that I climb the hill. As I strolled along, relishing the vivid foliage and the frosty air, I happened to glance down. The dove was on the path; one more step and I would have crushed it.

It was bright-eyed and alert, but made no effort to flee. I picked it up, chiefly to prevent my dog from grabbing it, and looked it over for several moments before I realized a wing was missing.

Had it been shot? Was it crippled by some hawk or other predator? There was really no way of knowing.

The incident, whatever it was, had not been recent. The wound had healed and the bird appeared to be faring quite well. It was as plump as most doves. The feathers were clean and preened.

I couldn't tell why it had allowed me to catch it; maybe it just was tired of walking. And I wasn't sure what to do with it. Could it survive on its own, especially with winter on the horizon, without being able to leave the ground?

To test it, I set it upon a large rock. It just stared at me. That inactive, it would be doomed, so I decided to carry it home and try to help it. But as I reached for it, the dove fluttered down to the ground and promptly marched off down the trail.

It seemed perfectly contented, almost natural, to be walking. It even walked like some of the ground birds, thrusting its

209

neck out with each step the way quail do.

There was so much confidence in its manner, I let it go, and wished it luck for the months ahead.

Over the winter, I thought of that dove occasionally when I was roaming around on the hill. I never saw it again, or found the tracks of a dove wading through the snow. There are foxes and owls and hawks up there to complicate matters, and the snow lay deep in the woods and the clearing for several weeks, so it was difficult to be optimistic.

Still, doves are surprisingly tough, and it could have survived. There were plenty of weed seeds available in the clearing, and the nearby cedars and hemlocks would have provided shelter as well as some food.

Now, I'm hearing a dove calling from that slope. It's probably not the same bird. There is so little chance that it made it through the winter. But I wonder.

Red-wings are special

We heard the sound as soon as we stepped outside that morning. It came from a distance, somewhere down in the bog. It meant spring had arrived. The red-winged blackbirds were back.

The red-wings are spring in the country. They are always the first of the migrants to reach here. When they arrive, the wave of birds coming up from the south is under way, and more will get here each day.

Grackles sometimes travel with the red-wings, and often cowbirds do. Belted kingfishers are early, too, and so are phoebes and killdeer and flickers. Robins and bluebirds are supposed to be among the leaders, but they're really in the second group.

But none are as early as the red-wings. They carry spring to the north on their shoulders, those shoulders that glisten with scarlet patches. Right now, only the males are here; they leave the womenfolk behind on these long journeys. For a couple of weeks, the males will hold their conventions in the lowland bushes and pasture edges, gossiping about the trip north and calling loudly— *awrrk-a-LEEE*—to anyone who listens.

The females are far less colorful—they resemble big sparrows, and not only don't have red wings, but they aren't even black birds—and they're quiet and unobtrusive. Nobody notices the females.

But everybody with ears knows when the males arrive. Their raucous chants are music in rural areas after a winter of silence. Other birds are tuning up, too; particularly song sparrows and cardinals and doves, but it is the red-wings who annually proclaim the transformation into spring. They not only add a new sound to the countryside, but they create a new feeling, one of carefree delight and resurgent life. As soon as the red-wings erupt into their "song," we can start looking for marsh marigolds and listening for spring peepers.

The red-wings reached our bog on March 5, which is a little later than usual. Last year, they came on March 3, the year before that on Feb. 27. In the 13 springs since we've been checking that swamp, the blackbirds' earliest arrival was Feb. 20 and the latest was March 7. Usually, they reach us in the last three days of February or the first three days of March.

Areas in the southern part of Rhode Island report red-wings considerably earlier, and there are always a few seen during the winter. We had one at our bird feeder on Jan. 1, but that was the only time we saw it all during the cold months. Those winter red-wings don't really count, anyway; it's the migrants that are so special.

Already, in just the few days since the red-wings arrived, the first phoebes and killdeer and kingfishers have reached us. The robins are on the way, and so are the few bluebirds that come up here these days. All will be duly greeted, each in its turn, but our biggest welcome is reserved for the red-wings. They are special.

Hunting the marsh marigold

This is the time of year when I go hunting. Not for rabbits or partridges, not even for mushrooms or wild fruits. Instead, I roam the swamps in search of the marsh marigold.

It's a wildflower, this marsh marigold, but I don't seek it out just to admire its petals. When I hunt for it, I'm hunting for spring, because no wildflower blooms earlier (don't count skunk cabbages—not even the most enthusiastic outdoorsmen would call them flowers). Finding marsh marigolds assures me—much like the red-winged blackbird and spring peeper do—that winter really has been defeated once more.

But it is not an easy flower to find. As the name implies, it is a plant of the wet places. However, it is seldom found along picturesque brooks or placid ponds. No, to find the marsh marigold, you have to get your feet wet; you have to push through the lowland brush, you have to be willing to sink up to your knees in the soft muck.

To be sure, some people do seek the marsh marigold for the table. Euell Gibbons, in *Stalking the Healthful Herbs*, recommends boiling the flowers' leaves for spring greens and even says the unopened flower buds can be made into a sort of pickle.

In addition, according to Gibbons, marsh marigolds are high in iron as well as vitamins A and C and supposedly are useful in treating all sorts of maladies ranging from epilepsy and anemia to warts. So herb fanciers collect the reclusive flower, too.

But not me. I stalk the marigold as eagerly as Gibbons ever did, but I don't pluck off a single leaf or petal. Just seeing the big, kidney-shaped leaves, greener than any summer plant, and the brilliant yellow flower glowing in the middle, is enough for me. I pause for a few moments, drinking in the sight, then wade back to solid ground. I'm satisifed.

Years ago, I first found the plants in a little, backwater slough deep in the woods. Each March I returned, and each time I was rewarded for my wallowing in squishy mud that sought to swallow my boots. I could always count on the marigolds, no

213

matter how bleak and endless the season seemed.

Then, most of the woods was bulldozed and much of the swamp was filled in for a building project. I saw it happen and resigned myself to the fact the shy flowers, hidden for so long from humans, were gone. I went looking elsewhere and eventually found a few marigolds in another marsh several miles away.

But, somehow, the bulldozers missed that tiny swamp in the woods. Parking lots and concrete and pavement replaced bushes and briars and mud on three sides, but the marsh marigolds survived. It still takes some pushing through brush and sloshing through muck to see them, but the dark-green leaves and golden blooms are still there. Every March.

And they still lure me back every year. The pull is as irresistible as the singing brooks on the hillsides and the kingfishers at the river and the tiny frogs chanting at the ponds.

One dream fulfilled

12-29-85 GOOD

A letter came the other day, a letter that was expected and looked forward to for several years. It showed that some childhood dreams are never forgotten.

Larry and I were boys together in Ohio. No two boys were ever closer. But he eventually went southwest, to St. Louis, and I came east. Now we see each other once every couple of years.

"Hi Ken,

"I am writing you while leaning back against an oak along the side of a stream that goes through my property. MY property. I camped out here last night and I've spent most of today just zeroing in and watching critters."

He did it, what we had planned all those years ago. He bought his own little wilderness. Then, of course, the plan was for us to be together, a couple of hermit bachelors with nothing but our trees and birds and "critters."

We spent our youth roaming Gib's Woods and there seemed to be no greater way to spend a life. By the time we were in high school, though, Gib's Woods had been bulldozed down. We would have to get our own wilderness, we decided, one that no bulldozer could ever touch.

"My woods is mostly oaks but also some pine, dogwood, redbud (in bloom), hornbeam and ash. There is an east-facing hill and a west-facing hill, each wooded and very rocky. In the valley between there is a stream flowing from north to south, and a flat wooded area of about 3-4 acres with a road going through it. This is the "backwoods" type of road common in Missouri, and, though public, is hardly ever used. So I'm going to call it my lane."

Larry has been pretty much a wanderer, spending his summers canoeing and backpacking all over the U.S. and Canada. Someday, he kept saying, he would find the perfect place. It would have hills and valleys and woods and water.

"I've found wild flowers in bloom here already; plantain-leaf everlasting, rue anemone, birdsfoot violets and bluets.

215

Mosses and lichens abound in the rocky soil and are more abundant than grass.

"Also, I'm keeping a list of birds I've seen here and have about 20 so far, in one day, including some you might be interested in; pileated woodpecker, brown creeper, goldencrowned kinglet, winter wren, bluebird, phoebe and wild turkey. The pileated and phoebe have nests here."

It was a book on birds that a relative gave me for Christmas when I was about 7 or 8 that really sparked this interest in the outdoors, first for me and then for Larry. A couple of years after I got it, when it was worn and dog-eared, I traded it to Larry for a box of baseball cards. He now has his own library of nature books, and a masters degree in earth sciences, but he still has that first book, too.

He's been teaching school for years but now he plans to go back to college. Technically, he'll be seeking a doctorate in botany, but he doesn't say it that way. "I have to go study some more. There are too many things I don't know yet."

If that's true, it isn't because he doesn't do his field work.

"Last night, during my first evening here, I sat out until the valley became dark and cold, then I climbed to the top of the east hill and sat in the sun a little longer. As I sat there quietly, I heard walking in the woods. I was expecting to see a deer but was surprised as a mink wandered on down to the stream.

"A little while later, a flock of turkeys worked their way through the valley. I came down the hill, had dinner, and then went for another walk. Again I found the turkeys (6 of them) but kept walking. Up past the spring, where calls of the peepers were loud, on up to the hilltop. There, with the full moon bright, I was treated to the show of a woodcock in mating flight. That's quite a way to get introduced to my new place, isn't it?"

A mink. Wild turkeys. Woodcocks. It sounds as though Larry has found his paradise. He used to lose all track of time just watching squirrels and chipmunks and soaring hawks back home. If there are wild turkeys and woodcocks on his hills, he may never come down.

"What do I plan to do with this place? Mostly nothing. I think I'll build a small pond and maybe, eventually, a cabin, but right now I don't even want to turn over a rock or a log. Basically,

I'll just watch critters.
"You're invited here any time. I'm going for a walk."

Larry"

By the time I finished reading the letter, I had developed a deep feeling of satisfaction and gratitude. It appears the dreams of one little boy are coming true for the man. I couldn't have been happier. You see, besides being my best friend, Larry is also my brother. So wait for me, Little Brother, I'll go on that walk with you.

A different drummer

Maybe this will be the year. It has to happen sooner or later, doesn't it? I hear grouse drumming every year; just once, I'd like to see the ritual.

Grouse—some people call them partridges—are fairly common in my area. I can find them nearly any time I want to. But I have never seen one drumming. That's the process by which a male attracts his lady friends in spring. He stands on a stump or log and beats the air furiously with his wings. Bird experts say it's something to see. So far, I've had to take their word for it.

Any time now, they'll begin. Usually, it's in the morning or evening, but in the very early spring, they may drum at any time of day. Roger Tory Peterson, in his *Field Guide to the Birds,* says the drumming "suggests a distant motor starting up. The muffled thumping starts slowly, accelerating into a whir: *Bup . . . bup . . . bup . . . bup bup up r-rrrrrrr.*"

That's pretty close. In fact, several times I hadn't realized I was listening to grouse at first. More than anything else, the sound resembles a small outboard motor. So if you're on the streams or ponds, fishing or canoeing, in the next few weeks, listen closely to that "motor"—it just might be a lovestruck grouse.

Last spring, I thought I had the grouse figured out. I was determined to find a drumming log and planned to keep my vigil until the bird cooperated. But they were too sneaky for me. On days when I couldn't sit around and wait, I would hear them. But when I was in position and ready, they refused to appear.

Later, I found a nest—with 12 eggs—beneath a little bush, and I tried to keep tabs on the birds for the rest of the year. They moved halfway up the hill by autumn, bursting out of the brush at the edge of the woods nearly every time I walked up there. In winter, I found their tracks, either in the dense hemlock thickets where they had plenty of shelter, or around the sprawling tangles of juniper in the rocky clearings where they could find meals of seeds and berries.

In recent weeks, they moved back downhill, lingering in an

219

abandoned apple orchard, where they fill up on buds while awaiting a permanent break in the weather. The buds they consume might produce apples, of course, and even though I sometimes gather a few apples from those trees myself, I don't mind the grouse helping themselves. They pay for what they take with their mere presence.

A grouse is a handsome bird, nearly as big as a chicken, with a colorful, fan-shaped tail and a crest atop the head that gives it an alert, perky appearance. Usually, however, all you get to see of a grouse is a blur of feathers after it explodes from the brush at your feet. That sudden flight is its defensive ploy, so startling predators—including hunters—that it often escapes while the pursuer hesitates.

Just a few days ago, I heard the hen-like clucking of the female grouse near the spot I staked out a year ago. There is a small clearing back there, and at the edge of the clearing is a decaying oak log. A perfect spot for drumming.

Maybe this will be the year I get to see it.

He just has to go

You can see him these days, out in the country, up on the hillsides. He's standing and listening. And he hears something that those in the city have a hard time noticing—he can hear spring coming. The countryman, or anybody in tune with the land, can hear it these afternoons, the sound of trickling water that can be the song of spring itself. Up there, among the trees and rocks and ledges, the thaw has begun. Spring has touched down.

A late snowstorm or a cold snap can make March feel as much like winter as January, of course, but now it takes a severe storm indeed to still those tumbling little brooks. Usually, they'll keep on running, right under the snow and ice, and if they are stopped, it won't be for long. Not now. Not in March.

Ask that man why he has to climb the hillsides each March, why he pauses so often and listens, and he probably would find his reasons hard to explain. But he knows he must go up there. He must pull on boots and whistle for his dog and make the annual pilgrimage. He just has to.

For the last few months, the hillsides have been quiet. There have been chickadees up there, of course, and passing visits by quarrelsome blue jays and crows, but on some days there has been almost total silence. The countryman who climbed there a few weeks ago would have heard only an occasional creaking of an old tree, maybe the rustle of leathery oak leaves, and perhaps the crunch of his own boots on the crusty snow. When there was no breeze, it was so still he could have heard the rocks themselves sigh in their slumber.

But now, the trickling waters are singing again, and there is no turning back. Even when all the snow and ice are gone, when there appears to be nothing left to melt and create the brooks, they will continue running for several weeks. The water is coming from the hill itself; it's the thawing of the frost that crept deep into the soil over those long months of winter.

It happens every year, and the countryman has gone to see it for decades, and even though it may seem the same each March, it is continually new and refreshing. It is a fundamental sound of the country, a milestone in the annual cycle of the seasons. He knows that when the hillside brooks break free, the thaw of his own fields and garden and yard cannot be far behind. And when the ground thaws, next come buds opening and seeds sprouting and woodchucks waking and orioles returning.

Eventually, about the time the first wildflowers appear, the brooks will cease tumbling. There will be no more frost to thaw, and the sparkling rivulets of March will become stilled, dried and forgotten. By August, the stepping-stone paths down the rocks will be hidden beneath leaves and bushes. And by August, the countryman will be busy elsewhere, noticing other happenings, and he won't be climbing the ledges as often.

But this is March, not August, and the hillside's lure is irresistible. Now, the man of the soil must climb up there and hear the song. Its message is so sweet. He just has to go.